# CHARLOTTE
## AND THE Starlet

## DAVE WARNER

RANDOM HOUSE AUSTRALIA

Random House Australia Pty Ltd
Level 3, 100 Pacific Highway, North Sydney, NSW 2060
www.randomhouse.com.au

Sydney   New York   Toronto
London   Auckland   Johannesburg

First published by Random House Australia in 2007

National Library of Australia
Cataloguing-in-Publication Entry

Warner, Dave, 1953–.
Charlotte and the starlet.

For primary school aged children.

ISBN 978 1 74166 124 8 (pbk.).

1. Games on horseback – Juvenile fiction. 2. Junior riders
(Horsemanship) – Juvenile fiction. 3. Horses – Juvenile
fiction. I. Title.

A823.2

Cover photograph by Getty Images
Cover design by SASO content & design
Typeset by Midland Typesetters, Australia
Printed and bound by The SOS Print + Media Group

10 9 8 7 6

*For Violet and Venice, who showed me the way to a girl's heart is a pony.*

# Chapter 1

The sun bore down from cloudless blue sky onto the red earth. Intense heat bounced in waves against the soles of Charlotte's boots as she strode past the expectant faces. She had spent almost every day of her thirteen years, ten months and six days in Snake Hills and today's furnace was nothing out of the ordinary. What was out of the ordinary was the throng of people, the noise and excitement. The Show came only once a year and nobody who lived within three hundred kilometres was going to miss it for the world. The crowd on the football oval was nothing like rush hour in the city but, compared to what was normal in this vast expanse of harsh country, the area could be described as jam-packed. Little kids jumped on plastic air-castles, parents and children fed ping-pong balls into the gaping mouths of plastic clowns and screamed with delight at winning a plastic water pistol, while in the background, the police band from Banebago Crossing played tunes that made old people smile.

In the mounting area, though, nobody was paying attention to anything except the other riders and their horses. Charlotte's new saddle gleamed on Stormy's back. When her father had led Charlotte into the lounge room last night while giving her yet another lecture on how to win the Golden Buckle, she'd been spellbound at the sight of the beautiful leather saddle. She had assumed he'd made it for himself.

'Wow, it's amazing. Can I hold it?'

'Of course. It's yours.'

She was too shocked to speak. Her dad picked it up and placed it over her arms. It was heavy and smelled divine.

'Well? D'you like it?'

She had put it carefully down on the couch and then thrown her arms around his waist, hugging him as tight as the nuts on his ute's wheel.

'It's really, really beautiful.'

She had felt so happy holding her dad. If only her mum had been there too, things would have been perfect.

⌒ ⌒ ⌒

The starter's command to take their mounts returned Charlotte to the present. The other riders couldn't help looking enviously at her saddle, which made her feel good. Dangling from it now was a small plush-velvet horse, a very special toy that Charlotte hoped would bring luck. She was the youngest rider in the race, but she knew she would receive no special treatment. Charlotte had ridden against these men and women informally many times while out on a muster and, at one point or another, had beaten them all. The cross-country was different though. This wasn't some quick, fun gallop from the hill to the gum tree. This was a prestigious event, and the winner was awarded the prized Golden Buckle. Her dad had won the race five times and she'd been dreaming of the day she'd be the one to bring it home.

She looked over her main competitors. Doug Evans would be tough. He'd been runner up to her father three times, including last year, and he would see this as his chance to finally break through. Sam Risto was only nineteen but he was probably the most naturally gifted horseman in the race. If he had a weakness, it was his tendency to take his mount over unnecessarily high jumps along the way. Becky Unly was the only other female in serious contention. She was a strong and smart rider with a wonderful mount.

Charlotte's father's voice broke in on her musings.

'Coming up that last straight the wind is very strong. You want another horse or two in front of you to shelter you a little, otherwise Stormy will tire.'

Charlotte couldn't imagine Stormy ever getting tired. But she nodded anyway to keep her dad happy. It was a shame she wouldn't be riding against him. His mount, Rocket, had injured a tendon and, for the first time in ten years, he would be a mere bystander. Mr Thomas, the official starter, called out in a loud voice. 'Riders to the start.'

Charlotte was excited, ready to win. Only one woman had ever won the race. That was her mum, the year before she got sick. Charlotte pulled herself up onto Stormy and moved into the line. Mr Thomas and her father went to either end and picked up a paper tape designed to keep the line of horses in some kind of shape.

'Ready.' Mr Thomas' voice was firm and clear.

Charlotte felt her heart begin to beat faster. She tried to fight the excitement. Her father had warned her not to worry about getting away quickly. So long as she didn't race too wide during the first lap around the oval before heading out to the bush, she would be fine. Charlotte was aware of the crowd becoming hushed. She sensed all eyes were on the riders and their mounts. The tape suddenly dropped and instinctively she drove Stormy forward as the crowd let out a big, whooping cheer.

There were twelve riders all up and it was likely that, at the end of the thirty minutes of hard cross-country riding, at least a couple would have retired. Charlotte was determined she would not be one of them.

The first lap was a blur, as if somebody else was on Stormy and she was hiding in her brain, looking through a keyhole at herself. She settled in the middle of the field, just behind Doug Evans. The next thing she knew they had left the oval and were heading out along the red soil track towards the bush. Stormy felt strong beneath her and she was dimly aware that a couple of horses were already falling off the pace, but she was determined not to look back. She noted a black horse up in front and guessed that would be Jamie Howard. Jamie always liked to lead, even in school running races. They turned into the bush, which was not much more than low scrub. Occasionally a fallen tree necessitated jumping, but it was nearly always a low obstacle. Doug Evans had edged away from her a little bit and she decided to hunt Stormy up by digging just a little harder with her heels. She was pleased that he responded effortlessly.

Tony Richards checked his watch nervously. The riders had disappeared into the bush twenty-four minutes ago and by his reckoning the leading horses should soon emerge, ready to sprint for the oval, where they would complete one final lap. He wished he were riding. Then at least he'd have something else to concentrate on apart from being worried for Charlotte. She was a natural horseperson but that was no guarantee against an accident, especially in a race like this. He imagined Julie giving him a stern lecture about letting Charlotte ride but then the thought vanished. Julie would never have forbidden Charlotte to do the thing she most loved, the thing she was best at.

A cheer went up from those people closest to the bush to signal the arrival of the leading horses and Tony's heart skipped a beat. His eyes scanned the line-up. Sam Risto was leading, Becky Unly was a length back and then . . . yes, there was Charlotte on Stormy, tracking Becky. About two lengths back came Doug Evans.

Charlotte felt confident. She was so focused she barely heard the cheering crowd greeting their return. About ten minutes earlier Sam Risto had gone to the front and quickened the pace. The horses had split into two groups. Stormy had responded well and Charlotte had found herself one of five leading horses. The leading group remained intact and now here they were back onto the oval for the last lap. One of these five would win.

Sam was about three lengths in front when Becky made her move to overtake him. Charlotte edged Stormy up behind. She sensed Doug Evans had not come with her and threw a quick look over her shoulder. Doug was dropping back a little, struggling. Coming up to the last turn, Becky sent her horse alongside Sam and then Sam's horse was drifting back towards Charlotte and Stormy, his race run. Charlotte moved around him swiftly. Becky had turned for the finish post, nearly two lengths in front. Charlotte panicked. Had she left it too late? She called on Stormy to give it everything.

Tony Richards watched as his daughter sent Stormy up on the outside of Becky Unly. 'She's gone too early,' he muttered, hoping he was wrong. Charlotte and Becky didn't look at one another as they called for their horses to give one last effort. Charlotte felt Stormy edge ahead of Becky's pretty chestnut. Just a little, and then a little more again. Yes! Becky's horse was beaten, just a hundred metres to win the Buckle.

Now that she was clearly in front, Charlotte could feel the strong breeze her father had warned her about. It was like an invisible arm pushing against her and Stormy. She could feel Stormy tiring. Not that it mattered. Becky's horse would be even more tired. And then she heard the crowd's shouting suddenly get louder and sensed something to her outside. She managed to turn her head just in time to see Doug Evans urging his mount on. He seemed to be flying. The winning post was so close she could even see where the paint was chipped.

'Come on, Stormy!' she urged. Poor Stormy tried hard but he was just that little bit too tired. Like a panther, Doug's horse reached Stormy a split second before the line. It was close, very close, when they crossed but she knew in that split second that she should have listened to her father. She'd been impatient and it had cost her the race.

# Chapter 2

A long way away on the other side of the world from Charlotte, a very frustrated man was trying to reason with another thirteen-year-old girl. The man was Tommy Tempest and he was a movie director, at this very moment on location shooting a movie. It was his job to help the actors understand what they needed to do and to make sure that the sound people, the lighting people and the camera crew all filmed the actors doing what they were supposed to do.

Tommy Tempest had directed three very successful films at the box-office, which all involved a young girl and her horse. The young girl was played by Sarah-Jane Sweeney, the thirteen-year-old who he was currently finding very, very frustrating. For every minute that they were talking and not shooting film, it was costing the film studio more than twenty thousand dollars. The film studio did not like losing money. If Tommy couldn't start shooting soon it might cost him his job. He tried to explain it once more.

'You don't actually fall, but it looks like you're going to and then you haul yourself back onto the saddle.'

Sarah-Jane blinked her baby blue eyes at him. 'I understand that, Tommy, but what's my motivation?'

Tommy was ready to scream. 'To win, Sarah-Jane, that's your motivation.'

Sarah-Jane pretended to consider that. 'Hmm,' she moaned doubtfully. 'But see, I won in *Spills and Thrills* when it looked like Amanda was a certainty to beat me and in *Dressage To Kill* I caught the murderer in the last stride. Can't we do something less . . . predictable?'

Tommy started what was soon to become a high-pitched wail. The only reason it didn't become a fully fledged yell was because he saw his assistant's worried face.

'What now?' Tommy snapped.

Mitch, the assistant, was used to his boss' moods. 'She's refusing to come out of her trailer.'

Tommy Tempest turned to Sarah-Jane, forcing a smile. 'With you in a minute, Sarah. Why don't you have a flavoured yoghurt or something?'

He pulled Mitch aside. 'Tell Leila we've got an *Entertainment Tonight* crew here. That always works.'

10

Mitch was deadpan. 'I already did. Nothing.'

ɔ ɔ ɔ ɔ

The movie location involved fields surrounded by thick woods. In a small clearing in the centre of the woods sat a very large trailer. The most modern and expensive that money could buy. From inside came the voice of a young woman. The sort of young woman who lives in Hollywood, parties a lot with celebrities and is used to getting her own way.

'Sarah-Jane thinks she can throw a tantrum and get them all running after her. I'll give them tantrum. I'll show them who the real star is.'

As she spoke, Leila studied herself in her custom-made mirror. It was the largest mirror in Hollywood, a town with many large mirrors. It needed to be that big to get all of her in. Not that Leila was grossly fat. But even a perfectly proportioned bay filly like Leila needed a substantial sheet of glass in which to study her reflection. And a vain one like Leila wanted to be sure she could see the sheen of her mane and the flare of her nostrils. She turned herself around, looked over her shoulder and studied the reflection of her butt.

'You can go on the treadmill all you like, Sarah-Jane, you can eat your lunch on it, you can even sleep-walk on it, kid, but you ain't never gonna have hindquarters like these.' Revelling in her superiority, Leila laughed to herself in a short, asthmatic whinny.

Feathers, a pink and white cockatoo who shared the trailer, looked down through the bars of his cage. Leila's ego was getting out of control.

'You want to be careful, Leila. That filly Chiquita is just waiting in the wings to take your place.'

Leila snorted through powdered nostrils. 'Chiquita? She can't understand human. When she hears Tommy talking about what he'd like the horse to do, she won't move automatically into position because to her it's gibberish. Little Leila, though, she knows exactly what they're wanting. Na, a few more hours and they'll be eating out of my hoof.' She turned her head to the side and studied her profile. 'Who's this new cameraman? Do you know what he's like? And what happened to Francesco anyway? Francesco was good.'

'Francesco got sick of you and Sarah-Jane's tantrums and found somebody easier to shoot.'

An inveterate gossip, Leila was curious. 'Who?'

'Russel Raven.'

Leila had heard about Russel Raven. He seemed to always be in trouble fighting somebody. His pictures didn't make as much money as hers but he was an Oscar winner. She liked the idea of starring opposite a real actor as opposed to that . . . brat with freckles. She felt she and Russ could push one another to new heights, whereas with Sarah-Jane she simply wanted to push her *from* very great heights. Still studying herself, she said, 'Yeah, well, the new guy better shoot my best profile or there'll be hell to pay.'

Feathers had had enough. 'There's no "best profile". You haven't been working out, you're eating junk. Look at this place.' He threw out a wing at a litter of empty fast-food cartons and soda cans. Leila had gone on another binge. 'There's only one way anybody could make your fat, ugly butt look good, and that's shooting it next to your fat, ugly face.'

'Watch it, no nose, or you might wake up with your claws glued to your perch.'

Feathers wasn't backing down. He'd known Leila since she was a foal. 'If your mother were here . . .'

If only Leila had a dollar for every time she'd heard that. 'But she's not, is she? She's off in Mexico or Madrid reading her fan mail and wasting her time with those stupid exercises, and playing up to all those past-it stallions.'

This made Feathers angry. 'You don't know what it was like for her. A single mom. She only wanted the best for you . . .'

'Oh, I had plenty of Swedish stablehands to look

13

after me while she was on tour, I know.' The hurtful memories still burned in Leila's brain. When she had been a vulnerable foal Leila hadn't wanted 'the best', just a mother beside her to protect and teach. But instead of being with her only daughter, her mother was always off headlining some show, dancing around the world in another exotic location. Hour after hour, day after day, little Leila had waited vainly for a glimpse of her mother but, as the shadows grew longer and Leila's hopes of ever seeing her mother faded like the light, she had grown harder, made herself less caring. Instead of her mother's heart beating beside her at night, Leila had fallen asleep to the sound of humans on television. Maybe that's why she understood human. Because the television had been her mom and dad.

'You don't know what you're talking about, Leila. Your folks had a tough life. Your dad working two-bit rodeos. Your mom doing double shifts on a dude ranch carting around tourists from Peoria right after the all-you-can-eat buffet. When they got their break in *Dances With Wolves*, even though it was just as a couple of cavalry horses, they seized it. They wanted the best for you. That's why your dad took on all the hardest stunts –'

'And that's what killed him,' snapped Leila.

'Exactly. So your mom felt it was all up to her.'

Leila didn't want to listen to any justification. As far as she was concerned she'd been abandoned. And it still hurt. Not that she would let anyone see that. She didn't want to ever be vulnerable again, and if that meant kicking somebody else before they kicked you, tough luck. She was going to show her mother that she didn't need her. She didn't need anybody. She was the prettiest, richest horse around.

She tossed her mane.

'Well, Mom doesn't need to worry about me now. I'm getting paid twice what she is for that dancing horse schtick in Vienna. And I have my own trailer.'

Feathers got back on course to where this had all started. 'You won't have it for long, the way you're going.'

Leila didn't believe that for an instant. She understood human language perfectly. Other horses might pick up a smattering here or there but Leila could actually talk human. Not that she'd ever let humans know. She was way too smart for that. If you were dumb enough to let them in on that little secret you'd wind up with electrodes in your head and a thermometer up your butt. So she kept her mouth closed and ears open. She would overhear Tommy the director talking and know exactly what he wanted. Then she'd give it to him . . . at a price. She admired her shiny bay coat in the mirror.

'Butter dipped in fur,' she purred.

'And the way you're going it'll soon look like lard dipped in vinyl,' Feathers cracked.

Leila was about to retort when she heard somebody approaching. As the door opened Leila dropped to the floor and made herself look ill.

Tommy Tempest entered. His face fell.

'Come on, girl, we need you.'

He squatted beside her and stroked her muzzle. Leila knew what was required to make him think she was trying to communicate with him. She threw her head around and blew through her nostrils.

What a ham, thought Feathers, watching the performance from his cage.

Tommy sighed. 'The vet says there's nothing wrong with you. I tell you, Leila, if I didn't know better, I'd think that you were trying to outdo Sarah-Jane. I know she can be difficult, but she's young and still learning.'

Oh, she's going to learn a whole lot more before I've finished with her, thought Leila.

Tommy Tempest stood, pulled out his cell phone and dialled. 'Joel? Tommy.'

Yes! Leila was pleased. Joel Gold was the producer, Tommy's boss. It was good that things were going to the highest level.

'Leila's very listless. I can't get her out . . . No, the vet says she's fine. He thinks she might be jealous. I mean, if she were an actress I'd just promise her top billing over Sarah-Jane.'

Whoa! Way to go, Tommy. Leila quickly got to her feet and trotted briskly out of the trailer, leaving Tommy thunderstruck.

'She just got up, Joel. Sometimes I swear she can understand what we're saying. I'll call you later.'

Tommy bounced back to the set. Things were looking up.

Leila quickly made her way to the make-up area and soon she was draped in her specially embroidered pink satin horse blanket, having mascara put on her long lashes by one of the make-up girls. Leila could never remember their names and why did she need to? She was the star. All she had to remember was numero uno. Next to Leila, another make-up artist worked on Sarah-Jane.

She saw Tommy jump up onto the flatbed of the open truck. A camera was mounted on the back. They were getting ready for the shot. Tommy called over to the make-up girls, 'Okay, standing by,' and suddenly everybody scattered, leaving Leila and Sarah-Jane. Leila felt the freckled brat mount her, but her eyes remained focused on the clapperboard.

'And . . . action!' commanded Tommy.

The board operator clapped it shut and Sarah-Jane dug her heels into Leila's ribs.

'Yaaaa,' screamed Sarah-Jane.

'Aaaaa!' yelped Leila to herself. She hated that. It hurt. And after all, she knew she was supposed to gallop as soon as the board clapped.

ᴐ ᴐ ᴐ ᴐ

Leila galloped hard towards the low hedge she was meant to jump. She could see one truck shooting in front of her and knew there would be one behind. Good.

'Move it, Leila,' Sarah-Jane yelled in that irritating high-pitched voice of hers, digging her heels in again.

I'll move it all right, you freckled freak, thought Leila. As she approached the hedge, she suddenly broke right and charged directly at a big oak tree with heavy, low branches. On her back she could feel Sarah-Jane fighting for control.

Time for the kid to 'branch' out. Leila drove Sarah-Jane into the lowest branch.

She heard the impact of Sarah-Jane's helmet on the

wood, and felt the sudden weightlessness as she tumbled off. Like the good horse she pretended to be, Leila came to an immediate halt. She turned and smiled, watching Sarah-Jane lying there, moaning. That would teach her to dig her heels in.

'People say it's hard to lose weight,' Leila tittered to herself. 'Nothing to it.'

The truck had stopped and Tommy and his crew had jumped out.

'Did you get the shot of her hitting the branch?' asked Tommy of his cameraman in a careful whisper.

'You bet,' came the reply.

Tommy could feel things going his way. That was going to look great on the big screen. And that moment when she hit the branch, that was one of the most satisfying in his whole life. There was justice in the world. He ran for Sarah-Jane, sounding solicitous.

'Sarah-Jane, are you okay?'

'No, I'm not okay. That dumb nag just ran right off course.'

With a degree of satisfaction, Leila looked over at Sarah-Jane shouting and throwing a tantrum. Good, Tommy wouldn't like that. Plenty of other freckle-faced kids waiting in the wings.

Leila would not have been so happy had she known that, at that moment, watching her from a distance were two men who saw in Leila not a beautiful bay filly but a large bundle of cash. One of the men was big and fat. He didn't wash very often and he rarely shaved so that his face resembled flypaper covered in dead flies. His name was Ralph. Right now, he was eating his third chocolate bar of the day. His friend was skinny with a face like a weasel. This was Bobby.

'You sure this is gonna work?' asked Bobby. He had known Ralph for a long time and while Ralph always had great ideas for easy money, they usually backfired. Like the time they were going to steal money from a vending machine. Bobby got his hand stuck in the coin slot and they had to get the fire brigade to cut it out. Then the police fined them and they had to pay for a new vending machine as well. But Ralph had no doubts about his new scheme. He tossed down the chocolate wrapper and wiped his sticky fingers on Bobby's shirt.

'Course this is gonna work. That horse is worth twenty million bucks to Joel Gold. You think he won't pay at least a couple of million to get her back?'

Bobby didn't answer right then as two paramedics walked past, carrying Sarah-Jane on a stretcher. She was screaming at them. 'Keep it level, you bozos, you're making me nauseous.'

Tommy Tempest was following his young star. He looked over to Ralph, who he knew as the plumber who supplied the requirements on location. 'You get the shower rigged yet?'

Ralph nodded. 'Yes, Mr Tempest, all done.'

When they were alone again Ralph whispered to his confederate. 'Just make sure, no slip-ups.'

Bobby hated the way Ralph acted as if he was hopeless. 'I told you, I got it all figured out.'

# Chapter 3

Feathers was dozing on his perch, dreaming of a far-off land where there were other pink and grey birds like him circling in the sky, squawking merrily. A particularly attractive female cockatoo was giving him the eye and now he was flying up to her, showing off, looping the loop and flying upside down. He could see she was impressed . . . then CRACK! Heck, somebody was taking shots at them!

Feathers woke with a start, momentarily losing his balance. He was forced to flap crazily to regain it. The sound, he realised with relief as he became fully awake, had come from outside the trailer and was not a rifle shot. It had been the sound of a twig snapping. Feathers looked out to see a skinny man sneaking through the woods. One glance told Feathers he was untrustworthy. Beady eyes. Never trust a man with beady eyes and the shadow of a beard . . . especially if he's sneaking through the woods.

This walking through woods was tough going. Bobby much preferred the nice, smooth concrete you got at places like racetracks. Who wanted trees and leaves and . . . Yuck! His lip curled as he realised he'd walked right into a spider-web. He clawed it off. It was only the thought of the money that made him carry on. Bobby checked his watch. The tranquilliser he had slipped into the security guard's coffee would have worked by now. He'd be out like a light. Bobby crept forward until he was only twenty metres from Leila's shower. The security guard was passed out. Everything was going to plan . . .

He stopped. What was that? There seemed to be some dreadful out-of-tune singing coming from behind the shower. Was somebody else in with the nag? Oh no, what was he going to do? Ralph was going to kill him. He might kill himself if that horrible racket kept up.

Luxuriating in the stream of warm water in her purpose-built horse shower, Leila was imagining that she was singing like her favourite singer, Kelly Clarkson. Well, actually, she thought she sang much better than Kelly. Singing came naturally to Leila. Maybe she'd put out an album . . . anonymously, of course. Just as she hit the high note, she realised that she was actually singing. Oops! It was the kind of thing that could get a girl out of sequins and into a hospital gown. She clammed up. She'd seen earlier that her security guard had fallen asleep but you couldn't be too careful. Somebody else might come by.

Leila could stay under that warm water all night but finally the thought of dessert dragged her out. The caterers did a fabulous chocolate mousse and she knew exactly when they arrived each evening – eight minutes from now. She stepped out of the shower and onto her special warm air-blower, which she could operate with her hoof.

Close by, Bobby said a silent prayer. The horrible screeching had stopped. He parted the bushes and saw the horse step out by itself onto its dryer. Good, whoever had been there must have gone. Time for the next stage of the plan. He reached into his bag, pulled out a warm pizza in a cardboard box and opened the lid. He looked in the direction of Leila's shower.

'Come on, baby,' he softly urged.

Her mane flowing in the warm air, Leila imagined

her film clip. She'd be galloping along a white beach. The song would be some rubbish about being in love in the summer sun.

Leila suddenly stopped and her eyes flew open. An aroma had crash-tackled her in the midst of her reverie. Mouth-watering pepperoni pizza. If there was one thing Leila couldn't resist, it was pizza. Especially pepperoni. Her nose told her it was close by. Maybe if one of the crew had it she could nuzzle him and he'd feed her a piece? It usually worked.

Like the children of Hamelin following the Pied Piper, she left the shower and trotted into the woods, following the scent.

From his cage in the trailer, Feathers saw Leila disappearing into the woods. He screeched at the top of his voice. 'No, you dumb filly! It's a trap. A trap!' But even as he shouted, he knew it was hopeless. Once Leila got pizza in her brain the only thing that would stop her would be a double-chocolate sundae with nuts. And right now he didn't have a double-chocolate sundae with nuts.

Leila followed the smell. It seemed tantalisingly close but each time she turned a corner, no pizza.

Finally she emerged into a small clearing. Bingo! There was a truck with the back down, forming a convenient walkway to where the pizza lay. She could almost taste it now. She trotted into the truck. Finally! There was the pizza, right in front of her. She was just about to take a bite when . . . BANG! Everything went black. For a second she thought somebody must have let off a bomb or something and she was dead, but then she felt the truck move. What was going on? Oh, now she got it, somebody had accidentally shut her in the truck. That was okay, when they stopped they'd let her out. In the meantime, there was nothing like pizza after a warm shower!

꒰ ꒱ ꒰

In the front of the truck Bobby was pleased with himself. Some people thought he was dumb but this time he'd proved himself pretty darn smart. Everything had gone one hundred per cent to plan. Of course, Ralph would say it was all his idea and give Bobby none of the credit he deserved.

The next part of Ralph's plan entailed driving the horse to the deserted soap factory. Bobby wasn't sure this was such a good idea. Let's face it, in every second movie somebody was hiding something illegal in some deserted old factory. If he were a cop, it was the first place he'd look for the horse. He'd tried to tell Ralph but Ralph just bullied him like always. Looking out of the truck window Bobby saw a field filled with horses. He suddenly had a very, very good idea.

Back at the scene of the crime, the police had been called. The security guard was still fast asleep, resisting all efforts to wake him. Tommy Tempest and his producer, Joel Gold, were tearing their hair out. Actually, Joel Gold didn't have any hair so he was grabbing handfuls of Tommy's hair and pulling that.

'We're ruined,' he wailed. 'Without Leila, we're ruined.'

Tommy mentioned gingerly that there were standby horses.

Joel Gold almost cried. 'Compared to Leila, they're just nags.' His cell phone rang. 'Joel Gold,' he mumbled, sniffing back tears.

A muffled voice said something.

'What? I can't hear you,' snapped Mr Gold.

On the other end of the line, in the cab of a truck littered with trash, Ralph pulled away the handkerchief he'd been using to disguise his voice. 'Listen to me, Mr Gold: we got the horse.'

The producer turned quickly to Tommy Tempest and whispered, 'It's the nag-nappers.' He spoke into the phone. 'Who are you?'

'Ra–' Ralph just stopped from giving his name. He saw Bobby smile at him smugly, as if he knew he'd nearly messed up. 'Rabbit. Call me Rabbit.' He gave Bobby a knowing smile, as if to say 'fooled you'. Then he turned back to the phone. 'I want four million.'

'Done,' said Joel Gold.

'Really?' Ralph was surprised and delighted as he peeled open another chocolate bar. 'We would have settled for two.'

'Okay, then,' said Gold. 'Two.'

Ralph realised he'd put his foot in it but it was too late now. He chomped on the chocolate bar. 'Okay, two it is.' He reached for the note he'd taken all night to write and read it out: 'Leev the monee in unmarked bills in the trash can by the Nantville exat Interstate 106.'

ↄ ↄ ↄ ↄ

'How do we know you have Leila?' Joel Gold wasn't a fool.

'You'll find a slice of pizza with the impression of her teeth in it, outside your trailer.'

Joel Gold felt queasy. He'd eaten that piece of pizza when he got the news of the nag-napping. It was a sort of nervous response. 'So, where is she now?'

'In a disused factory,' said Ralph confidently. Then he noticed Bobby waving frantically. 'Hold on a second.'

Ralph put his hand over the phone and turned to Bobby.

'What? What's up with you? You want to go to the bathroom?'

'We need to talk,' hissed Bobby.

Ralph had a bad feeling.

'I'll call you back,' he said and hung up on Joel Gold. His eyes bored into Bobby. 'What have you done?'

Bobby smiled confidently. 'It's okay. Don't worry. I thought of a much better hiding place.'

Leila did not like the way this had turned out at all. One minute she's eating pizza, the next she's turfed out into this cold paddock. The open air, mind you! At night! Surrounded by all these aggressive low-life horses. The ringleader, this black stallion, a real thug, was crowding her now and the others were starting to close in too. There didn't seem to be anywhere to run. Was this some last-minute scene Tommy had come up with?

Leila put on her foxiest smile, the one she flashed at all the paparazzi during premieres.

'Hi guys, you looking for autographs or something?'

They stared at her blankly. Surely this crew knew who she was? Was it conceivable horses wouldn't know the most famous celebrity of their own kind? She tried to move off.

'Guys, nice meeting you but I gotta get out of here. I got a pedicure booked tomorrow.'

She tried to squeeze through but they narrowed the gap. The black stallion whinnied loudly in horse language. 'You sound like a two-leg. Speak horse.'

Leila was nervous. Better do what the guy says. She put on the best throaty, hoarse tone she could muster. 'Okay . . . I gotta get out of here, I got a pedicure.'

The black stallion reared, angry, and whinnied again in horse: 'You think you can mock me? Cut it out, speak horse!'

Oh, he means *horse*, not hoarse, she realised.

It had been so long since Leila had spoken horse. She was nervous. She tried to slip into her best approximation of common horse but only managed a pathetic whinny. The other horses laughed at her. A grey mare was particularly cutting. 'What a bimbo! A two-day-old foal can speak better than that.'

Another horse, who sounded like he'd spent too much time in the open, taunted, 'Looks like she needs a few lessons. Let's give her a really good one.'

Now Leila was very scared. The black stallion led them towards her, nudging her with his muzzle, forcing her to back up. Maybe a bit of inner city patois would work? She tried to recall how cool rappers sounded in their movies.

'Hey, come on, sis, bro! We're all quadrupeds, right? Let's drop the temperature a little. I got a nice Prada feedbag back at my trailer. You guys can have it. Or how about a set of Ferragamo shoes?'

She showed them her horseshoes and grinned her biggest, friendliest smile. Confident she'd turned them round, she waited for their response.

They lunged at her.

Leila let out a squeal and started running as fast as she could towards the other side of the paddock. Why had she been bewitched by pizza? Why hadn't she stayed in her trailer? Where was Mr Gold?

She hadn't gone a hundred metres when she started wheezing. Her legs buckled. That no-neck Feathers had been right – too much pizza, too little exercise. Her legs were very wobbly now. Where was a stunt mare when you needed one?

Suddenly lights struck her full in the face and she was flooded with relief. Ah ha! It was a trick after all. Tommy must be back there shooting some night scene. She hadn't noticed this scene in the script. Come to think of it, she'd never actually got around to reading the script this time. Anyway, what did it matter? She was a star. Now she could tell these uncouth equines what she really thought of them. She turned on the grey mare.

'Hey grandma, the feedbag? Forget it. Prada, nada. As for the shoes, you'll be wearing them all right, right across your plain, grey muzzle.'

She expected to see Tommy, the cameraman and the lighting crew but, as the lights grew brighter, she realised they were just the headlights of a truck. A very big truck with the words INTERNATIONAL LIVESTOCK written down one side.

Leila still wasn't worried. It looked like they'd sent a stretch limousine to pick her up.

⊃ ⊃ ⊃ ⊃

Speeding down the road, Ralph couldn't contain his

anger. He shouted at Bobby, who was hunched beside him.

'You changed the plan?'

The old truck with RALPHS REMOOVALS AND PLUMMING painted down the side veered to the wrong side of the road for a moment as Ralph slapped Bobby with his greasy, duckbill cap.

'Look out!' yelled Bobby.

There was a massive truck heading right at them. Ralph jerked the wheel just in time to avoid colliding with the big rig, whose driver angrily honked his horn at the much smaller truck.

'You're getting upset for nothing,' wailed Bobby. 'Come on, somebody finds a nag in a factory, they know it's suspicious, but in a paddock? No-one's going to notice one more horse. You'll thank me for it.'

But ten minutes later as Bobby and Ralph stood in a deserted paddock, Ralph was not thanking Bobby. He was on his knees crying and beating the ground with his fat fist.

'Why? Why in God's name did I ever have to meet this imbecile?' he moaned.

Bobby was slowly backing towards the truck. Any second now Ralph would blow.

'Aaaaaarrrggggh!' There it was. Ralph's mighty

bellow like a wounded bull. Bobby started running, knowing Ralph would be right behind him ready to whack him with that duckbill cap.

ᴐ ᴐ ᴐ ᴐ

Meanwhile, the big INTERNATIONAL LIVESTOCK rig powered along the road and in the back, a certain glamorous horse was trying some fast-talking.

'Come on, guys, I was joking!'

Leila tried her most winning smile but she might as well have fired a peashooter at a tank. The grey mare looked especially unimpressed. The horses moved in still closer, threatening.

Leila held up a hoof. 'Okay, okay . . . I'll give each of you a Mary-Kate and Ashley CD, personally signed.'

For a moment she thought it had done the trick. And then the black stallion powered in at her and somebody trod on her hoof.

'Careful!' she yelped. 'That hoof is worth its weight in . . . Yow!' Some horse had trodden on her other hoof. She hoped that, wherever they were going, this trip would be short.

# Chapter 4

That night, after the Golden Buckle race, Charlotte and her father were doing the washing up in the small kitchen of their weatherboard farmhouse. It was actually Mr Thomas' house but as head stockman, Charlotte's dad got accommodation as part of his pay. They'd lived there her whole life. Tonight her dad had cooked shepherd's pie, her favourite dinner. That made her feel even more guilty about not having listened to him before the race. Tonight he seemed more quiet than usual. She presumed he was annoyed with her, though he had said nothing more about her riding tactics and had even given her a double scoop of rainbow ice-cream.

'A letter arrived for you yesterday.' He said it in an offhand manner as he methodically rinsed off soap bubbles. Charlotte felt her stomach contract. There was only one letter it might be.

'From the JOES?' Being part of the Junior Olympic

Equestrian Squad had been her dream ever since she'd first learned about it at the Banebago gymkhana a year ago.

'Uh huh.' He plucked an envelope from the top of the chugging, noisy old fridge and handed it to her. It was just a rectangular bit of paper but, to her, it felt as heavy as a boulder. The contents could make her leap to the sky with joy or want to crawl into a hole in the ground and lie there for a month.

'I didn't want to distract you from the race,' her father was explaining, but she barely heard him. In truth, she had not ever expected it to come to this. A man attending the gymkhana had identified himself as a talent spotter for the JOES, and he'd recommended Charlotte apply for the introductory course, a one-month camp held more than a thousand kilometres to the south of Snake Hills, where promising young riders were evaluated. At the end of the camp there were trials, with the best riders offered a permanent place in the JOES elite development squad. Over the next two years they would hone their skills, competing both nationally and internationally. The very best of these were likely to become Olympians.

Charlotte's father had helped her fill out the form and, a few months later, Mr Graham, the head of the

JOES, had flown up to see her ride. He watched her closely but gave nothing away, informing her she would hear something within the next six weeks.

And now she held the answer in her hand. Charlotte stared at the envelope. Nothing to be afraid of, she told herself. So she wouldn't get chosen, big deal, this was a good place to live and her father could teach her everything about being a stockwoman. She ripped open the envelope.

Her eyes found the line straight away.

Immediately all the strength went from her legs and she plopped down on a chair. She looked up wanly at her dad.

'Hey, it's okay. There's always next year.' He stroked her hair, consoling her.

Her voice was weak and seemed to come from a long way away. 'I'm in.'

◡ ◡ ◡

The next week was a blur. The cost of the camp, which ran during school holidays, was much more than her dad's savings. Mrs Thomas wouldn't hear of Charlotte missing out, though. She organised quiz nights and raffles, and made the whole town chip in. And now it was almost time to leave. Charlotte stared at the dry, dusty plain that seemed to stretch on forever. She felt very empty. She'd miss her dad terribly, even if it were just for four weeks.

'I'll miss you too, Stormy.' She patted the big chestnut horse on which she sat. She would even miss this scorching, hot piece of land. It was more than home; it was part of her. She knew every dip in the plain, every rock on the hill and just about every lizard hiding under those rocks. She would miss her friends but she supposed she would make new friends at the riding academy. After all, they were all girls who loved horses, so they would have that in common.

Charlotte dug her heels into Stormy and felt exhilaration as the big beautiful beast tore across the red earth, turning the dead air into a breeze that danced around her face. This was heaven, this moment, her body shuddering with each powerful stride. Here, nothing could touch her. Here she was complete.

∪ ∪ ∪

At the cattle yard, Tony Richards saw his daughter galloping towards him. She was a natural horse-person. This invitation to try out for a place in the JOES was a chance in a lifetime and no matter how much it hurt to be without her, he would not do anything that might give her cause not to go. Julie would have been so proud to know their little girl had been selected for a trial.

This was their last day together before Charlotte left him for the first time. If she made the elite development squad then she would spend most of the year away with the JOES. Even if she didn't, he knew that when she came back she could be changed forever.

Charlotte came to a halt beside him.

'So what would you like for dinner tonight?' he asked, already knowing the answer.

Charlotte forked down the last morsel of mince and potato, realising that she hadn't even thought about what food they might have at this Thornton Academy, where she'd be boarding. She hoped they'd have top food like her dad's shepherd's pie.

'You packed?' her father asked.

'You know I am,' she said.

She saw him smile and realised he'd been teasing her. She'd packed days ago!

'What I meant was, have you got more things to pack?'

Charlie didn't normally correct her father. 'No, it's all done except for my wash-bag.'

He smiled some sort of secret smile and walked out of the kitchen. When she didn't move he poked his head back in. 'Come on.'

She joined him in the lounge room. At first she thought he was holding a shiny tent. Then she realised it was a satin dress. The awful significance of it revealed itself before her father even spoke.

'Mrs Henderson made it for you. She said the satin is very good quality and came from a bridesmaid's dress. How about that?'

Charlotte swallowed hard. It was horrible. Not that she knew much about fashion. She'd had some party dresses when she was little but since then she had worn only jeans or shorts. As they didn't have television up here it was difficult to tell what sort of dresses thirteen-year-old city girls wore but she was certain they did not resemble this . . . thing! In Rockhampton the nurses had kept bringing in big glossy magazines for her to read to her mum. Charlotte had loved the new smell of the shiny paper. But she'd been disappointed by how pathetic and soft the girls in the photos had been. They always had hair like velvet and skin like milk. No way would they be able to endure a two-week muster. They did wear pretty dresses, though.

She stared at the shiny sail again and the anxiety she felt about leaving started to blow up like a willy-willy.

'It's lovely.' She knew this untruth fell into the category of lies you were allowed to tell. 'But I won't need it, Dad.'

'Actually, you will.' Her father handed over the dress. It had a lot of lace tacked around the bottom so that the overall effect was of a costume for a giant kewpie doll. 'The letter said you'd need clothes for social occasions.'

Her anxiety became panic.

'What social occasions?' She hadn't bothered to read that part of the letter.

'I think they have a party to welcome all you girls.'

Charlotte's panic subsided. That wasn't too bad.

Her father continued. 'And I think there might be a dance or something with the boys' academy.'

Boys! Oh, no. Charlotte didn't mind working with boys, she didn't mind playing football or cricket or softball with boys but *dancing* with them? This was ridiculous. Wasn't this Thornton Downs place for learning how to jump and do dressage? What did dancing have to do with that? Charlotte's history with boys was patchy to say the least. When Brian

Buchanon thought he'd scare her by putting a snake in her schoolbag, she reacted in the only way a real girl could. She belted him in the nose. For the rest of the day she had to stand staring at the classroom wall. Not that she minded. Everybody laughed when Brian walked into the classroom from sick-bay with a big, stupid bandage around his nose. She would have stared at a wall a whole week for that moment. Maybe this dress was karmic payback.

Her father said, 'I'm glad you like your dress. You better brush your teeth and get to bed. We've got a long, long drive. Nearly sixteen-hundred k.'

She offered to help with the dishes but her dad wouldn't hear of it. She reached up and kissed him goodnight, fighting the urge to cry.

'See you in the morning.'

It was dark when Charlotte woke and checked the old clock radio by her bed. Two a.m. Three hours before they left. There was something she needed to do one last time. She got quietly out of bed and tiptoed into the lounge room. Making sure the sound was low, she clicked on the TV and the video player and then inserted the tape which had inspired her to want to be a JOE. It showed a beautiful young woman competing in an equestrian event. The young woman's face shone with excitement as she moved her mount effortlessly around the ring. The young woman was her mum. She'd been competing at the Royal Show in the city, aged twenty. It was when her mum and dad had first met. He had been down there looking after cattle. When her mum's horse escaped, he recaptured it, riding bareback. They fell in love instantly. Her mum had told her that story a hundred times and, even after she became ill, whenever she told it she always laughed and looked twenty again.

Something inside Charlotte had come alive at seeing that video of her mother. Everybody always said what a great rider Charlotte was and she knew she was fast and could jump as far as any boy, but she wished she could be as graceful as her mother had been. Her dad had told her that her mum might have ridden in the Olympics if she hadn't married him and moved to the middle of nowhere. This was really why Charlotte wanted to try out for the JOES – to be like her mum, to make her proud and pay her back in some way for what she had given up.

# Chapter 5

It is often said that people resemble their pets. A man walking a Pekinese is likely to be rotund and waddle. Siamese cats are favoured by sleek young women who enjoy soaking up the warmth from the sunniest window of their apartments. Miss Caroline Strudworth of Thornton Downs Equestrian Academy had spent her entire life around horses and, to be frank, it showed. Over six feet tall in her riding boots, which she wore the entire day except when in bed, her face was long, her nostrils slightly flared and her mouth was crammed with teeth the size of bathroom tiles. And when she laughed it was with a decided whinny. A lack of grey hair suggested an age less than fifty but her attitudes belonged to somebody in their sixties. On rare occasions she could act quite girlish, but most of the time she ran her academy the way Captain Bligh had run his sailing ships, with an iron fist. Today she was trying to occupy herself while awaiting what, for her, was the highlight of the year – the new intake of horses. Like a child on Christmas Eve, she had barely slept last night and had been up as usual at five a.m.

Miss Strudworth was extracting troublesome weeds from around the base of the parade ground flagpole when her acute hearing snaffled the hiss of hydraulic brakes, the way a frog's tongue might lash out and snatch a fly mid-air. The lorry had arrived and was slowing to negotiate the gate at the foot of the drive.

A minute or so later she reached the stables, her heart beating fast. Bevans, the stable foreman, was already at the big lorry chatting with the driver. His gaze turned on Miss Strudworth as she arrived.

'Chap here says he's got thirteen horses. I told him we only ordered twelve.'

'That is correct, Bevans.' Miss Strudworth was certainly not going to pay extra. She pulled out the invoice from a stiff tweed pocket. 'I have the invoice right here and I'm not paying a cent more.' She handed it across to the driver.

He checked it against his order and shrugged. 'It's the same price. Maybe they threw in an extra one, like? Baker's dozen?'

Bevans pointed out that Hero, the colt, was still struggling with colic and an extra horse would be handy with the new intake of JOES due to arrive today. Miss Strudworth had learned from great-grandfather Tobias, founder of Thornton Downs, to never look a gift horse in the mouth.

'Very well, so long as it's not costing me anything,' she said.

She noted the first of what would be a long line of Mercedes, BMWs and those absurd four wheel drives arriving at the gates. The intake comprised fifteen girls, all proven horsewomen. Over thirty days they would hone their skills under Miss Strudworth's watchful eye. After this they would compete in the disciplines of dressage, jumps and point-to-point, and then seven would be selected to return as full-time members of the squad.

Miss Strudworth knew that while the girls might arrive with the same hopes, they would not all leave with them intact. For those who succeeded there would be boundless happiness; for those who missed out, utter despair. A pity, but that was the way of the world. As Miss Strudworth herself knew, it was a very foolish person who believed in happy endings for all. Somebody always had to miss out. She thought of her lonely trophies up there in her parlour. Yes, sad but true, somebody had to miss out. Her gaze drifted to a large Mercedes where the

Hayes-Warrington girl was climbing out.

'Yes, Mum, no, Mum, bye, Mum.'

She slammed the door. A beautifully groomed blonde was getting out of a BMW next to her. She was talking quite angrily to somebody in the car.

'. . . and if pizza face uses my computer while I'm away, I'll set fire to her pigtails again.'

Miss Strudworth took a deep breath. Thirty days of having to deal with these precocious princesses would test her. But life, after all, was not meant to be easy. She would emerge triumphant as always.

ↄ ↄ ↄ ↄ

Leila had no idea where she was. The last thing she remembered clearly was being in a field and a big truck arriving and bundling her in with the 'hacks'. Then somebody had jabbed a needle into her and the next thing she knew she was being led out of the truck with a dozen or so other nags, including that bundle-of-fun-not grey mare.

'Hey, nanna,' she managed in horse. 'Where are we?'

The grey mare narrowed her eyes. 'What's it look like?'

'It looks like the set of every movie I've ever made.'

'We're in a riding academy.'

A riding academy! Ludicrous. 'I don't want to ride, I want to eat.'

The grey mare shook her head in disbelief. 'No you idiot, *they* ride *us*.'

She inclined her head to the gaggle of teenage girls who had congregated in the centre of the circular driveway.

Oh yeah? Leila smirked. She'd like to see them try and ride her, she really would.

ᗡ ᗡ ᗡ ᗡ

Miss Strudworth ascribed the success of her academy to careful selection of horses. Some she sourced in Australia, some came from Europe and some from her favourite breeders in California. Her program of putting young riders and horses together in an equestrian symbiosis had won plaudits, not just from Mr Graham, who ran the JOES program, but internationally. While most of the girls attending would have their own horses back home, Miss Strudworth had set in place a rule that at Thornton Downs all the girls would start equal. They would each choose a new Thornton Downs horse and bond with that horse over the course of their stay. In this way she felt that girls from less advantaged back-grounds were on something of an equal footing with their wealthier peers. Miss Strudworth looked over the array of inductees and blew her whistle loudly.

'Girls,' she commanded in an imperious voice, 'your rooms are listed on the board in the foyer. Place your bags in your rooms and return immediately to the stables to select your horses.'

The girls moved off briskly. Those who had been here before knew that the right horse could make or break your chances of making the JOES elite squad.

כ כ כ

Caked in red dust, the battered old station wagon swung up through the high stone arch of Thornton Downs. Charlotte tried not to show that she was worried about arriving late. Her poor dad must be so tired. Thornton Downs was almost at the other end of the country to Snake Hills and he had driven all day yesterday. They had slept in the car before setting off again before dawn. Unfortunately, not long after starting this morning they had hit a steer. The impact had created a leak in the radiator and her dad had been forced to make running repairs.

The only upside was that Charlotte got to chew a lot of gum so her dad could push it into the hole in the radiator to stop the leak. It worked but the car had kept overheating and they'd had to keep topping up the water, which also slowed them down.

For the last hour or so of the drive Charlotte had been sitting with her mouth open. The land here was so different to Snake Hills. The fields were lush and as green as the tracksuits of Australian athletes. Thornton Downs itself left her speechless. Even her father let out a low whistle. Charlotte drank in the crisp white fences that surrounded the paddocks. Everything seemed neat. Everything seemed perfect. In the near distance, she could make out a circle of smooth dirt with hurdles and steeples around it. This was the real deal. Thick bush bordered the paddocks. A flock of exotic parrots shot across the sky, squawking loudly.

She was so excited but also a little nervous. How could she ever belong in a place like this? That feeling deepened when the massive main building loomed into view.

Three stories high, gabled and built of neat red brick criss-crossed by white piping, the building totally dominated the landscape. Compared to this, even Mr Thomas' house looked like a doll's house. Directly in front of the main building was a large parade area of unblemished clay. Wow. She just knew she was going to get lost here.

There didn't seem to be anybody else about as her father pulled to a stop near the building. Charlotte had already said goodbye to Rusty the cattle dog, who sat in the back seat moaning as if he knew he wouldn't be seeing her for a while.

'Explain we're late because we hit a steer.'

Charlotte nodded and gave her dad a final hug.

'I guess it's time,' he said simply.

'I guess it is,' she said, and let go.

'I'll ring you,' her father promised.

'You better.'

She managed a smile. She knew that she had to go that instant. If she stayed any longer she'd burst into tears. She quickly kissed her dad, hooked on her backpack and walked towards the big building. She counted to one hundred before she turned back to see the rusty old car covered in thick red earth just turning away and back onto the main road. This was it.

She had almost reached the door when a voice boomed out.

'Where do you think you're going?'

It sounded like a man's voice. Charlotte looked around but could see nobody.

'Up here.'

A severe looking woman was hanging out the window.

'Isn't this where you are supposed to come?'

The woman frowned. 'It is if you're on time. But you're late.'

'We hit a . . .'

But before Charlotte could explain the woman thrust a long arm out the window and pointed to some large sheds about half a kilometre away.

'To the stables. Now. Get your horse. The other girls are already there.'

Charlotte didn't dare argue. She dropped her backpack and ran as fast as she could.

༄ ༄ ༄

The stables were very large. Eight horse stalls down each side with two tack rooms, one in the middle of each side. There was also a small open office where Bevans and the vet had a desk to work from.

The other girls had selected their horses and were already grooming them, oiling up their tack and gossiping. Lucinda Hayes-Warrington had long, lustrous black hair and had been riding since she was six. Emma Cross wore a blonde bob, which was also lustrous, and she'd won many pony club events. Rebecca Portofino had thick curls of red hair but otherwise her life was pretty much the same as the other two. Like them she lived in a house so big she could go days without bumping into her parents. And their beach house was even bigger. Not quite as big as Emma's father's beach house located in the next bay. That had been so big that locals had taken up a petition saying it blocked the sun on the beach. What with skin cancer and everything, Emma said they should have been grateful to have some shade.

Emma was showing Rebecca and Lucinda a brand new mobile phone no bigger than a snack pack of sultanas. It was her going away present from her parents.

Lucinda groaned. 'Honestly, a mobile phone. Haven't they any imagination?'

Emma waved off her concern.

'No, this is actually pretty cool. Rhinestone touch-pad, waterproof of course, world-wide coverage, global positioning beacon, digital camera with, natch, storage for one hundred and ten snaps, seven-language diary, calorie counter and karaoke function. Plus. . .' She pointed to tiny microphone holes at one end. '. . . the eavesdropper. So sensitive you can hear conversations a kilometre away.'

Rebecca said she had wanted that model but her father had said she would have to earn it. 'I said, no way am I doing the dishes.'

Emma shook her head in sympathy.

'Pathetic, isn't it? My dad tried that too, once. I said, "Daddy, you're not the only one trying to buy my affection. I can easily get that from my step-father."'

Rebecca noticed a shabby looking girl enter and look around. Obviously the stablehand. As she passed, Rebecca spoke up.

'Could you oil my gate, please? It's got this annoying creak.'

The girl looked at her blankly.

'Can't you do it?' she replied.

The three friends swapped a look. Talk about attitude. Rebecca was not to be cowed.

'That's what stablehands are for, isn't it?'

The girl shrugged. 'I'm not a stablehand.' As her father had always taught her to do, Charlotte extended her hand. 'Charlie.'

The three girls looked at her as if she was an alien life form. No-one made a move to take her hand and Charlotte pulled it back, feeling embarrassed.

'Emma, Lucinda, Rebecca,' said the one with the blonde bob and the three of them turned back to their horses.

Charlotte didn't know what to do next. She felt foolish standing there and had no choice but to push on. She walked to the end of the stable, looking for a free horse. There wasn't one. A man she took to be the stable foreman was placing tack on one of the hooks on the wall.

'Excuse me, I don't seem to have a horse.'

Bevans didn't even look at her.

'Try the second-last box on the left.'

Charlotte was sure she'd walked down there already but she went for another look, just in case. The stall door was closed. There was no horse standing above it. She was about to go back again when she thought she heard . . . what was that? *Snoring?* She pushed open the gate gently and there lay a beautiful bay filly on her back, fast asleep.

'Hello, beautiful. I'm your new best friend.'

The noise woke Leila. She had feigned sleep while those annoying riding kids had come around looking for horses to torture and must have drifted off for real.

Now some kid was pushing some geeky smile into her personal space.

'We better give you a name. Let's see . . .'

Leila could almost hear the hard drive whirring in the girl's mind. Britney, she was going to pick Britney . . . oh no, anything but Britney.

The girl smiled down at her.

'Cher. I'm going to call you Cher.'

CHER!!! Leila almost choked.

'My mum had all her CDs. She thought she was fabulous.'

This rube obviously had never met Cher, thought Leila, who vividly recalled the studio confiscating Leila's trailer for Cher's second bedroom.

'Okay, Cher, let's get acquainted.'

Couldn't the kid just buzz off and leave Leila alone? Leila let one eye flip open, shuddered at the rat's nest hair that confronted her and closed it again. She'd go away. Now, where was that dream she'd been in? That's right, it was Oscar Night and she was partying with that cute, Irish . . .

EEEEEEEE!

Leila was suddenly wide awake, covered in something cold and . . . WET!!!

Water.

The last time she'd been hit with anything that cold

was playing water bombs at Hilary's pad. Hilary, now there was a good little comrade to party with. Of course, the water that time had been chilled Perrier. But this wasn't Perrier, this was common garden variety $H_2O$. Leila stood quickly and shook herself dry. And that's when she saw the rube smiling at her, holding an empty bucket.

'Thought that might get you awake. I'm Charlie.'

No, kid, thought Leila, you're dead meat.

The girl started drying her off. Mmm, well, that was as it should be. She was rough, though, nothing like those Korean girls in the bathhouse near the studio. What did she think Leila was? Horsemeat?

'You're a pretty girl, aren't you?'

Duh. Course I'm pretty, you doofus.

'A bit podgy, but we'll get that off you.'

Podgy! From the look of her, this rube clearly didn't even know how to use a cleanser or a lip-liner. And here she was calling Leila *podgy*!

'Tomorrow I'll take you for a canter and we'll see how you handle the jumps.'

Leila smiled at the naivety. Charlie thought she was the boss? Well, let's see how she handled the old face-slap.

Whack! The horse's tail swatted Charlotte hard in the face.

Charlotte was stung. It was almost as if the horse had done it deliberately.

'I hope that was an accident, Cher,' she joked.

Whack, whack! This time, two swats.

'Oh, it's like that, is it? Then let's see how you like the bridle.'

If there was one thing Leila hated it was a bridle. But she didn't react. She let the kid get close. It was a ruse Leila had used effectively in *Hoofbeat Hero* when the bad guy was trying to escape from the police on her. You relax, get them confident, then just as they lean in and smile, like the rube was now, you suddenly butt them in the chest.

Caught completely off guard, Charlotte was knocked backwards, her legs collecting something behind her. She tumbled over the stool and hit the ground but it wasn't as hard as it should have been. It was soft and squelchy and foul smelling. Yuck! She had landed slap in the middle of a pile of horse poo.

She had just gotten to her feet when the horsy woman with the deep voice entered. She looked down her very long nose at Charlotte.

'Finish up here, girls,' she announced. 'Dinner in forty-five minutes.'

It took Charlotte a good five minutes to hose herself off. Then she had to find her room. In awe, Charlotte entered the large lobby. The floor, a dark red-black polished wood that smelled of wax, squeaked under her sneakers as she headed for the room allocations, which had been pinned on a notice-board at the foot of the most magnificent staircase Charlotte could have imagined. The other girls had vanished into the cavernous maw of the building by now, though she could hear the occasional door bang somewhere up above.

Charlotte located her name. She'd been allocated the Princess Grace room with three other girls. Charlotte noted the floor plan: upstairs, down the corridor to the right, second room on the right. She hoped her room mates were friendly. Slowly she climbed the staircase, savouring every step. There were pictures all along the panelled walls. Many were of men in red coats with big moustaches, on sleek horses. Then pictures she recognised as being of the British royal family. She passed a couple of other girls running down corridors but they didn't acknowledge her. Eventually she arrived at the Princess Grace room and could hear lots of excited girly chatter coming from inside. She stepped in and her heart sank.

Sitting at dressing tables crammed with beauty jars, hair straighteners, curling wands and hair dryers were the three girls she had encountered at the stables.

# Chapter 6

Tommy Tempest walked to the trailer and knocked gingerly on the door. Inside he could hear Mr Gold sobbing. Sniffling, Mr Gold opened the door wearing his big quilted dressing gown and slippers embroidered with his initials, though tonight they were on the wrong feet. He hadn't shaved and his eyes were red.

'Any news?' he asked hopefully.

Tommy Tempest shook his head. 'Leila has vanished. The police say there's nothing more they can do.'

This provoked a new bout of sobbing from Mr Gold.

'This is costing me a fortune.'

Tommy Tempest knew Mr Gold wouldn't want to hear the next bit but he had no choice.

'We need to get another horse for the part. Leila could be in Timbuktu by now.'

Leila looked over the barn. What a dump! She could be in Timbuktu for all she knew. No sign of a plasma, not even a cappuccino machine and, by the looks of it, she was expected to sleep on hay! She could hear those other chumps hoeing into their oats as if it was devil's food cake. Pathetic. At least there was no sign of that black stallion. What a bully! This crew of nags were still giving her the cold wither but big deal, like she cared? Anyway, Mr Gold and Tommy Tempest would be on the case, they'd track her down. Until then, Leila was going to sit on her backside and do a big fat nothing. These schmucks were all excited about jumping over a fence. What the heck was that going to get you but a broken fetlock? *Jumping over a fence!* What did they think she was?

For an instant, the image of her mother gracefully dancing in a big ring and leaping fearlessly over high steeples came to her. Leila got a big lump in her throat. But only for a moment. Life had taught her to fight those emotions. She had cared for her father and he had died doing a stupid movie stunt, and she had cared for her mother and been left alone with nannies and television while her mother had gone off with a bunch of show ponies. She would not allow herself to be hurt again, uh, uh. She had hardened her heart like thick oats mixed with water and left in the sun. Her mother would be lying around in a spa in Palm Springs getting a pedicure, with a bunch of compliant pintos nodding away at her as she talked her head off about 'the tough old days at the dude ranch'. So it was tough – get over it, lady! No point living in the past.

Leila lay down on her hay. Damn, it was itchy! She longed for her wonderful rubber mattress with the electronic back vibrator, for a well-made smoothie and, yes, she hated to admit it, but she longed for Feathers, that no-neck lump of sinew and fluff. She shut her eyes. Maybe when she opened them up it would be just like it was before – a big spacious trailer with Leila being treated the way a star ought to be . . .

ᴐ ᴐ ᴐ

Charlotte anxiously checked the clock on the wall of the Princess Grace room. In five minutes she was supposed to be dressed and at dinner and here she was still in her underwear waiting for the bathroom, clutching her towel and baby powder. Already dressed in a very simple but gorgeous frock, Rebecca was blow-drying her hair. She hadn't been too bad. Just ten minutes in the shower. Lucinda had taken even less time but was still applying make-up. Charlotte had never seen so many products. Mr Jedley, the chemist at Goondowi Downs, didn't have so much in his whole shop.

The real problem was Emma.

'My father is a barrister.' Lucinda added a touch more mascara. Lucinda had been talking about where they lived but Charlotte hadn't been paying attention. Some suburb in the city Charlotte had never heard of. 'I guess you know Emm's papa is John Cross, who owns all those TV stations?'

Charlotte shook her head.

'What does your father do, Charlotte?'

'He's a stockman.'

Lucinda brightened. 'Oh, Rebecca's mother and father are both brokers. Mervin-Lynch or something, isn't it?'

Rebecca shrugged. She was having particular difficulty with her lip-liner.

'No, no,' said Charlotte, understanding the mistake they were making. 'He's a stockman. He rounds up cattle.' She could see the other girls trying to comprehend. 'On a cattle station.'

There was a pause as the information wriggled into the narrow room that was Lucinda's brain and flicked a switch. 'Oh!'

Rebecca swung to her, still confused. 'What?'

'Like a cowboy,' translated Lucinda.

Rebecca nodded slowly. 'Right.'

'Does he own the station?' asked Lucinda.

'No, Mr Thomas owns it.'

Lucinda and Rebecca looked at each other for guidance. Rebecca smiled at Charlotte.

'Doesn't matter, I suppose.'

Charlotte hadn't ever thought there was anything the matter with that, but for some reason she felt obliged to add, 'He's the head stockman.'

'Mmm,' the others hummed in unison.

Once more Charlotte felt quite uncomfortable. These girls weren't easy to be friends with. She wanted to retreat. Fortunately that opportunity was provided when the bathroom door finally opened and a huge cloud of mist poured out. Emma emerged through it, wrapped in a towel.

'Sorry, Charlotte, but if you don't wait a minimum of seventeen minutes between the conditioner and the course2 shampoo you just don't get the sheen.'

Charlotte felt an urge to give Emma's head a course2 wash in the toilet bowl but she told herself it was important to make friends, so she simply smiled and slipped into the bathroom.

As soon as she'd gone, Rebecca switched off the

hair dryer and said she felt sorry for her. 'I mean, *baby powder*! I haven't seen that since . . .' She thought a long moment, then brightened. 'Since I was a baby!'

Lucinda shuddered at the thought. 'Obviously she's poor but in my book there's no excuse for not at least having a cleanser, scrub and foundation.'

The others nodded at the truth of this fact. Emma slid into her designer outfit. 'To think for a moment there I was feeling guilty about using up all the hot water.'

In the shower, Charlotte shivered. It was only partly because the water was freezing. It was equally nerves at having to change into that frock for dinner.

# Chapter 7

'Chicken broth . . . pot roast . . . apple crumble . . . Where's "eye of newt"?' Rebecca dismissively flipped the menu away. She, Emma and Lucinda were seated at one of the long wooden dining tables where they would eat their meals over the course of the next few weeks. Crafted from hardwoods that had travelled from the south-west of Australia by bullock and dray, oaks that had been shipped from England in steamers, and maple that had wound its way from Canada, the dining room of Thornton Downs was solid, cavernous and dark.

Just the way Miss Strudworth liked it. Old Tobias had employed wood carvers to work horses' heads into the picture rails all around the room. A giant oil painting of the old man himself – with his mutton chop whiskers, ruddy nose and suspicious eyes that looked as if he'd just caught a greengrocer weighing his potatoes with trick scales – dominated the front of the room.

From her platform beneath that flinty gaze, bouncing on the toes of her pristine riding boots, Miss Strudworth looked over the students and felt her pride swell. This was her vocation: to take these girls and give them not just a better seat, but a better path to life as young ladies. Oh yes, Miss Strudworth knew that was an old-fashioned concept in these days of wireless phones and ordering vegetables over the internet. She *was* old-fashioned. Frankly, she was proud to be. Just because much of the modern world had gone to pot didn't mean Thornton Downs had to follow the example.

'Old Dudworth is looking more like a horse than ever,' observed Lucinda, doodling on the back of a form she'd found on the table. The caricature featured a horse in jodhpurs with an unmistakable facial resemblance to Miss Strudworth.

'Did you guys know that Todd Greycroft is our neighbour?' Emma dropped the bomb casually in their midst. As one, Lucinda and Rebecca fell upon it.

'Todd Greycroft's at Milthorp?'

They spoke in unison with exactly the same reverent tone. Milthorp was the boys' riding academy, the equivalent of Thornton Downs.

'He's a god!' Lucinda's jaw was almost on the table.

'His family is so rich their servants have servants,' said Rebecca in awe.

Lucinda announced, 'Well, when we mingle with the Milthorp boys, I'm setting my sights on little ol' Todd.'

Emma rolled her eyes. 'Please. The only way Todd Greycroft would spend time with you was if he was selling zit cream.'

Lucinda smiled back brightly. 'You're right. You've got a much better chance. He does a lot of charity work with the handicapped.'

Rebecca's attention was on the table of girls at the front of the room beneath Strudworth. 'Those girls are talking about us.'

Lucinda shrugged. 'Oscar Wilde said it's much better to be talked about than to be caught wearing last season. Or something like that.'

Rebecca snatched Emma's phone off the table. 'I want to hear what they're saying.'

She inserted the earpiece and cranked up the volume on the 'eavesdropper' to full. It was rather unfortunate timing. Just as she pointed the phone at the table of girls, Strudworth cracked her riding crop loudly against her boot. Rebecca's eyes crossed then rolled back into her skull. She managed to pull out the earpiece just as the crop once again snapped against leather. Miss Strudworth spoke as she had been taught in many elocution lessons. Clearly and loud.

'Welcome to Thornton Downs. As you know, this is an opportunity for you to showcase your skills and win a place in the JOES. But matters equestrian are not all that is important. While you are here I will expect good manners, camaraderie and . . .' As she spoke Miss Strudworth noted the large door at the back of the dining room creak open and a latecomer make her way in. She stopped cold and glared. '. . . punctuality.'

Charlotte tried to move as silently as possible but each step she took on the wooden floor sounded like a gunshot, with the gun pointed right at her heart. Her shower had lasted two minutes, leaving just enough time to get ready, but then she had spent a good two minutes staring at *that frock*, wishing that it would magically change. It was so ugly compared to the clothes the other girls had but she had nothing else to wear besides jeans, and the note had specifically said jeans were not permitted at dinner. Besides, her father and the people of Snake Hills had meant well.

She still might have made the dining room in time but she had never been in such a big building and she took several wrong turns before finding her way. Now with each step she could see Miss Strudworth's frown more clearly. She could feel the looks of the other girls turning on her. Then she became aware of giggles and suppressed laughter. Her skin started to feel prickly and hot.

The colour drained from Rebecca's face.

'Oh, no. She's been sick on her clothes.'

'No, that's the dress,' hissed Lucinda.

Emma said it would help with her diet as it had put her off her food.

When Miss Strudworth resumed speaking it was with a bark.

'You, young lady, are . . .'

Charlotte imagined herself in front of a firing squad with Miss Strudworth having just yelled 'fire'.

'Charlotte Richards,' she said.

'That may be your name but what you *are* is late. Take your seat.'

Charlotte slunk in beside Rebecca, feeling the size of a half-chewed peanut.

'As I was saying,' continued Miss Strudworth, glaring at Charlotte, 'I place particular store in manners. You may be the best horseperson in a saddle but I'm afraid if you fail at matters of character you will not make the JOES. At Thornton Downs our motto is . . .'

Those who had previously been through the

academy chanted like ancient druids, 'The family that rides together has pride together.'

Strudworth smiled, pleased. 'Exactly. Enjoy your dinner.'

᠔ ᠔ ᠔

The meal passed without event. Charlotte enjoyed the roast. Lucinda, Rebecca and Emma talked among themselves and, to be honest, Charlotte didn't understand half of what they said. It seemed to be in some foreign language. Rebecca tried to include her, asking her what her favourite TV show was. When Charlotte said they didn't have TV in Snake Hills, Emma assumed she meant cable, whatever that was. Charlotte said no, they didn't have TV at all.

'So what? You just hang around the mall?' asked Lucinda, as she played with a grape.

'Mall? You mean shops?' asked Charlotte, who had never seen one but had heard girls at school talk about them. The other girls nodded eagerly: finally she understood!

'Yes, shops. You know, Smart Girls, Backchat, Vixens, Rave, Argument, Trolly Dolly, Mucus.'

Charlotte didn't know any of these shops. She

explained that in Snake Hills there was just the hardware shop, which doubled as the stock and station agent, the newsagent that doubled as a post office, and the general store that doubled as an electrical shop.

The others were stunned.

'So they do have electricity?' asked Emma.

'Most of the time,' said Charlotte.

'But what about clothes shops?' Lucinda couldn't quite believe this third world stuff she was hearing.

'People make their own clothes.'

'Oh.'

Emma couldn't think of anything more tragic. Having nothing to add, she swung back to Lucinda and Rebecca and reignited their conversation about cute tops, skirts and accessories. Not wanting to just sit there like a dork, Charlotte picked up her plates and took them to the kitchen. Emma shook her head disapprovingly as Charlotte disappeared.

'Now she's cleaning up!'

Rebecca sighed. 'That's sooo cheap.'

When Miss Strudworth noted the Richards girl helping stack dishes and taking them to the kitchen, she felt a twinge of remorse for scolding her. In all the years she'd run the academy, Miss Strudworth could not once recall one of the students helping the kitchen staff like that. She herself had done it – old Tobias had expected children to help. Miss Strudworth realised now this was the girl from the cattle station in the outback. Perhaps the girl had simply got lost en route to dinner? Miss Strudworth prided herself on her fairness. She would not put a black mark against her name just yet.

Returning from the kitchen, Charlotte heard Miss Strudworth slap her boots with her crop again and silence quickly descended.

'On your table you will find a form that absolves Thornton of any blame should you be killed, maimed or put on weight during your time here. Sign it and hand it to the right.'

Determined not to be last this time, Charlotte snatched a form and began filling it out. Strudworth continued as the forms were passed forward.

'Most of you will not make the JOES. Sadly, as those four crazy mop-tops from Liverpool once sang: we can't all get what we want. If you do make it, well done. If not, don't wallow in self-pity. Move on and do something at which you might be better. We can't all be champion equestrians any more than we can all be happy brides sharing toast and marmalade with a handsome Master of the Hunt.'

'What's she on about?' hissed Rebecca.

'Being an old maid,' Emma hissed back.

Lucinda was about to join in when a cold fist of fear seized her heart. The cartoon she'd done was on the back of a form in Strudworth's hand, which she was waving around as she spoke. Lucinda had been entirely ignorant of the fact that her drawing paper had been a form that would be handed up. Strudworth would kill her. Unless – she felt the tiniest glimmer of hope – because it was on the back of the form, maybe she wouldn't notice?

That slim hope was dashed when the girls at the front table began pointing and laughing. Strudworth stopped, followed the trajectory of their eyes and found the cartoon. Her mouth tightened. Lucinda's stomach knotted.

'Girls, get changed for bed. We have a big day tomorrow.' Strudworth shook the form with her fist. 'Charlotte Richards, I wish to speak to you.'

Lucinda was stunned. Obviously Charlotte had accidentally picked up the form she'd doodled on. She wondered for a second if she should say something. Emma read her mind and gripped her wrist.

'Don't be stupid. Charlotte's not going to make the JOES anyway.'

Lucinda guessed she was right and she quickly left with the others.

Charlotte assumed she had made some mistake in filling out the form but she had no idea what that might have been. She shuffled forward to the front of the room.

'Yes, Miss Strudworth?'

Strudworth flashed the drawing in her face.

'Where you come from, Richards, being cruel may be considered humorous, but at Thornton Downs there is no place for this cruelty. I hope your horse-womanship is better than your art. Dismissed.'

Charlotte tried to speak in her defence.

'But, Miss . . .'

'I said dismissed, Richards. Six a.m. sharp, parade ground, dressed and ready to mount.'

Charlotte turned on her heel, angry. The others had set her up. She'd tried to be friends with them but if they wanted war, she would oblige.

Catching them at the top of the stairs, Charlotte ran past them, blocking their way. 'Which one of you did that cartoon?'

Lucinda shrugged. 'I didn't mean Strudworth to see it.'

'You do that again, you'll pay.'

Emma joined in. 'Get over it. That poor-kid, Eminem-chip-on-the-shoulder-thing doesn't cut it here, Charlotte.'

Lucinda piped up. 'We're privileged and proud.'

The three off them pushed off again.

'I'm not finished yet,' Charlotte called angrily, but when she went to go after them she tripped on the enormous satin monster she was wearing and went sprawling onto the hard wooden floor. While she'd had many worse tumbles from horses, the embarrassment was dreadful. The Evil Three, as she now thought of Lucinda, Emma and Rebecca, turned back to her and laughed their heads off. Charlotte picked herself up, slowly. This time she gave them plenty of time to get away from her. She was already missing her dad, Stormy and Rusty. Thirty days of this would be hell.

ᗡ ᗡ ᗡ ᗡ

Leila shifted uncomfortably in her stall. This straw was the pits. If only there were cable, at least that would help pass the time. It was like watching treacle spill in here. Mmm, treacle! Leila smacked her lips. What she wouldn't do for a stack of pancakes. Well, one thing she wouldn't do is jump hurdles or prance around like a window dresser on Melrose. She caught the grey mare looking over at her with a superior gleam in her eye.

'What are you looking at, Greybeard?'

The mare whinnied, 'You don't belong here.'

'For once you ain't talking drivel,' she shot back.

'You're a lazy spoiled brat. We're equestrian horses, we're proud of what we do.' The mare turned her back on Leila and the other horses followed her lead.

Leila shook her head. Like she cared. Her whole childhood she'd been on her own so the silent treatment was no big deal. Still, she couldn't stay in this dump. If Joel Gold or Tommy didn't show up soon, she'd have to phone them. But then, she didn't know the number to call. She relied on Feathers for that stuff. Where was the scrawny piece of avian fluff when you needed him?

ᗡ ᗡ ᗡ ᗡ

A morose Feathers was sitting on his perch wondering where Leila was and trying to figure out how to give these dopes a clue about the bad guy he'd seen the night she disappeared. Okay, so Leila was a pain in the tailfeather, vain and self-centred – but there were mitigating circumstances, as Feathers was only too well aware.

For a start, after Leila's dad had died in that horrible accident, Leila's mother had become very protective of her. She hadn't ever been allowed to mix with other horses in case she got an infection or something. Instead her mother would sneak her into the shack where the stablehands watched TV. Something happened with that TV exposure because one day Leila started speaking like a human.

Well, her mom had flipped! She was happy for her daughter because it opened up a whole load of possibilities but, at the same time, she warned her never to reveal to humans that she could talk. Leila's mom was doing a dancing show at the time and she made sure Leila got all the showbiz tricks she needed: how to mug to camera, how to toss your mane just so, how to suck up to the director. But she was a working mom and her work took her away for long stretches. She was away when Leila got her first big role, and of course Leila slayed them in the aisles.

Next thing she's got a mountain of chocolates, her own spa, a massage bed. Naturally that's going to go to a young filly's head. And a lot of it was Leila wanting to get back at her mom for what she saw as deserting her.

Still, Feathers had never given up hope on Leila. He was sure she just needed the right catalyst to make her

79

understand what was truly important. Now, though, she was gone. Feathers felt very, very sad and worried about how he would break the news to Leila's mom. He wondered if they would ever see Leila again.

# Chapter 8

Next morning at five-forty-five, Charlotte was already dressed in her new riding clothes. She liked the feel of the tailored jacket and jodhpurs, which had ironed assiduously. No way would she give Miss Strudworth an excuse to fault her today. But she couldn't find her boots anywhere. She was certain she'd left them under her bed last night after polishing them to a bright sheen, but they weren't there now. She spent ten minutes looking everywhere she could think of. Now she was growing worried. The Evil Three were dressed and heading out.

'Have you seen my boots?' she asked in desperation.

She noted the sly flicker of a smile on Emma's lips.

'You're not suggesting we did anything to them, are you?'

And Charlotte knew then that they had.

'What did you do with them?'

She saw Lucinda and Rebecca scuttle out but Emma stood her ground.

'You're so paranoid, Charlie.'

Charlotte would have loved to have punched her then and there but she couldn't afford the time. Where had they put her boots? She had searched the bedroom and bathroom. Her gaze slowly settled on the window. She threw it open and looked down on the parade ground below, where some girls were already assembling. She couldn't see any boots. And then she noticed the big tree right in front of her window. She looked up.

There they were, wedged high in the branches. She checked her watch. Four minutes to six. She had no option but to try and get them.

She climbed up onto the window sill. It wasn't that far to jump to the nearest branch but it was a long way down if she slipped. Taking a deep breath, she pushed off with all her might.

She felt the thrill and terror of sailing through the air before gravity began to pull her down. Her hands shot out and wrapped around the closest branch, but the momentum was too great and she began to slip. In desperation she dug in with her fingernails. She held, dangling high above the assembly of girls. Gradually she worked her palms into a more secure position and then summoned her strength and swung herself up and onto the branch. Safe. She breathed a sigh of relief.

The boots were about three branches above and, even on tiptoes, Charlotte couldn't quite reach. She would have to climb to the next branch. She started scaling the trunk, using her knees and hauling herself up. She could see Strudworth on her horse directly below and hear her urging the girls to fall into a straight line. Charlotte started out along the next branch, straddling it like a witch on a broomstick. This bough was nowhere near as sturdy as the first one. She edged very carefully, the branch bending under her weight. She daren't go any further for fear of it snapping, but if she lay along the branch and stretched, she might just reach.

She tried. Nearly . . . She stretched a little more and her fingers encircled the heel of one of the boots. She started to drag it towards her, a centimetre at a time. It was going well until it hit a bump in the branch and slipped from her grasp. The second boot went with it. She watched helplessly as they dropped like bombs, zeroing in on Strudworth's head.

Oh no. She was about to score a direct hit on the boss!

At the last second Strudworth's horse moved

forward and the boots slammed down behind her. Miss Strudworth turned back quickly and scanned. She was sure she had heard two quick thuds but there was nothing in sight. It must have been her imagination. She checked her watch. Right on six. She raised the whistle to her lips.

Up above, Charlotte began to relax. It could have been so much worse. Now, if she could just wriggle back to her room . . . CRACK!!!

She was falling through the air before she realised the branch had broken. The ground was rapidly rising up to meet her, although she was actually heading for the water tank.

She hit it dead centre, at the very instant Strudworth was about to blow her whistle. The good thing was that the water broke Charlotte's fall. The bad thing was the obvious one. She was now soaking wet. Charlotte fought her way to the surface of the tank. As the water drained out of her eardrums the first thing she heard was the gale of laughter from the assembled riders. Even though it hadn't been her fault, she wished there were some way she could just burrow down into the earth and hide there for a hundred years. She contemplated remaining in the tank but knew that too would only make things worse.

Slowly she pulled herself up. The sight that

greeted her made her wish she had merely been hung, drawn and quartered. Miss Strudworth was still seated on her horse but she was absolutely soaked. Water dripped off the peak of her riding helmet. Her face was stone.

'Sorry, Miss,' mumbled Charlotte, as she dropped down from the tank to the ground and retrieved her boots. Charlotte was aware the other girls were trying to avoid eye contact with her in case they got tarred with the same brush. As she put on her boots she saw Strudworth try to write something on her clipboard. The paper was so wet it ripped.

'Stables,' commanded Strudworth. But when she tried to blow her whistle all that came out was a bubbly burr. Charlotte didn't dare look back as she ran hard to get her horse.

ᔅ ᔅ ᔅ ᔅ

Leila was considering what she would give right now for a half dozen croissants when the gate flew open and the rube, soaking wet and looking like the creature from the black lagoon, threw a bridle over her. Leila fought hard but the kid was a whole lot stronger than she looked. Before Leila knew it there was a saddle on her back, bright and new and actually quite classy and then – aaaahhhhhh – Leila had to breathe in quickly as the cinch strap snapped around her belly. She fought with all her might but the bridle couldn't be resisted and, centimetre by centimetre, she felt herself dragged out of the stall, through the stable and out to the parade ground, where the grey mare and the rest of the horses were standing in a straight line like the palm trees on Wilshire Boulevard.

ɔ ɔ ɔ ɔ

Miss Strudworth watched the Richards girl struggling with the filly. She doubted she would last a week.

'Riders, mount!' she commanded and all the girls mounted with alacrity and poise, except for Richards, who was having a devil of a time with the pretty bay. 'Just a light canter around the property.'

The girls moved off efficiently with one exception; Richards' mount was doughnutting like a hooligan in a V8 doing burnouts on a lawn.

ɔ ɔ ɔ ɔ

Charlotte was frustrated and would not let Cher win. No way. She finally broke out of the doughnut and into a canter. She hoped that would be it now, that she had established who was boss.

ᔐ ᔐ ᔐ ᔐ

To Leila, this was just another Sarah-Jane in different clothing. She'd got rid of one, she would get rid of the other. She suddenly broke for a tree with low branches, just like the one that had Sarah-Jane seeing stars.

ᔐ ᔐ ᔐ ᔐ

Unlike Sarah-Jane, Charlotte was a true horsewoman, not an actor who could ride a bit. When she saw the tree coming at her she dropped straight back like a limbo dancer, the bough passing over her nose.

ᔐ ᔐ ᔐ ᔐ

Leila couldn't believe it. The rube was still on her back. How was that possible?

But Leila had many more tricks up her saddlecloth. She began galloping after the other riders and then, just as she felt Charlie relax, she hit the brakes.

ᔐ ᔐ ᔐ ᔐ

The sudden stop caught Charlotte by surprise and she flew over the horse's head and landed hard on her backside. As she struggled to her knees, she could just see the other riders disappearing in the distance. Cher was standing there, smugly.

'You horrible, wretched, stupid beast,' she said as she dusted herself off.

'If I'm so stupid, how come you're the one picking dirt out of your teeth?' the horse replied.

Without thinking, Charlotte snapped back, 'You had the element of surprise. You won't get that again.'

The horse was dismissive. 'Pull your breeches down, your voice is muffled.'

'Very funny,' said Charlotte. 'You can't even talk. You're a horse.'

Charlotte folded her arms triumphantly, convinced she had won the argument. And then it dawned on her what she had just said. This was a horse. It couldn't talk. She must be imagining it.

'No, you're not imagining it,' said the horse, as if reading her mind. 'I could talk a whole lot better if you took this stupid bridle off.'

Charlotte pinched herself. She could feel it clearly. Okay, she wasn't dreaming. But there must be a logical explanation. She must have bumped her head when she fell. Anxiously she felt over her head for blood.

The horse spoke again. 'You didn't fall. I threw you.'

Charlotte shook her head. She closed her eyes and counted to ten. Then she slowly opened her eyes. Cher seemed to be standing impassively where she had been before. Tentatively, Charlotte advanced towards her. With each step she took she felt more confident that she had imagined the whole episode. Cher continued to stand there, not moving. Now she was right beside her. Charlotte sighed with relief.

'I was imagining it.' She stopped to pick up her helmet.

'No you were-en't,' came that annoying sing-song voice.

Charlotte almost jumped out of her skin. No, this was not happening.

The horse spoke up again. 'Will you hurry up and get this bridle off? Come on. I'll tell you all about me.'

Without understanding what was truly happening or why she was doing this, Charlotte complied and removed the bridle.

'Much better,' said the horse when it was off. 'By the way, the name is Leila. Not "Cher". And while I've got your attention let's lay down a few ground rules: I want burgers or pizza, none of that corn and hay stuff, I am not to be disturbed before midday and never,

ever plait my mane. Now if you'll be so good as to find a phone and call my producer . . .'

The words were just a fog but Charlotte picked out the word producer.

'Producer?'

'Don't you recognise me? I'm a movie star, for goodness sake. People say it was J-Lo made curvy butts fashionable again – uh uh. She got the idea after she saw me in the powder room at the Four Seasons. I don't mind, though, me and J-Lo are like that . . .'

The horse who called herself Leila crossed her legs. She continued. 'And take a look . . . Familiar?' She turned three hundred and sixty degrees, modelling.

Charlotte thought she could see a vague resemblance. 'Barbie's Star?'

Leila nodded proudly. 'Of course, they screwed up the legs, much too chunky. Look at these pins. Now, can you tell me exactly where I am?'

By now Charlotte was no longer resisting. She felt like Alice in Wonderland, embracing the madness.

'Australia.'

'I've never been interested in skiing but the après-ski bar had always appealed.'

'I think you're talking about Austria.'

Leila's eyes went the size of softballs.

'Australia! That place with killer spiders and . . .

CROCODILES!!! Oh my God, I'm going to die. I'm going to die.'

Charlotte folded her arms. The horse could talk but it clearly wasn't that well read.

'There aren't any crocodiles in this part of the country.' She saw Leila relax and took great pleasure in adding, 'Snakes and poisonous spiders, yeah.'

'SNAKES!!!' yelled Leila. 'This is like being on *Survivor* without the cameras.'

ɔ ɔ ɔ ɔ

Later, as they trudged back to the stables, Charlotte was still shaking her head.

'A talking horse. No-one's going to believe this.'

'Exactly. 'Cause you're not going to tell them. And even if you did, who is going to believe a rube like you?'

'Rube?'

'Yeah. Doofus, schmuck, nancy no-friends. They won't believe a word you say.'

Charlotte couldn't understand her attitude.

'Think of how famous you'd be.'

Leila pointed out she was already famous. 'You think I need hypodermics in my butt, electrodes in my brain and a lot of egg-head scientists prescribing a low-fat diet? I'd be ready for the padded stall before you could crack your whip. I'm sorry I even opened my big mouth.'

That annoyed Charlotte.

'You can trust me, you know. In fact, we have to be friends if we're going to make the JOES.'

Leila had had enough. She didn't need friends, she needed an agent. And a little chilled strawberry milkshake wouldn't go astray.

'Think you can rustle up a "shake du strawberre"? I'm parched.'

Charlotte decided not to respond. Okay, a talking horse was amazing but, if she thought Charlotte would play the servant role, she had another think coming.

The other girls had long since arrived back and now, as they came within the immediate vicinity of the recreation area, Charlotte could smell barbecued sausages and hear the strains of 'Kumbaya' floating over the field. When she got closer she saw Miss Strudworth was strumming an acoustic guitar enthusiastically, bellowing out the vocals like an auctioneer at the cattle sales. All the girls had earphones in and were listening to those iPod things. Charlotte would have killed for a sausage.

'I hope you're happy. I haven't eaten all day and now I'm too late for the barbecue.'

'Believe me, you could do with a couple less pounds.'

Charlotte led Leila to the stables, removed her saddle and began brushing her.

'Up and to the left,' commanded Leila.

'We have to talk about the JOES,' began Charlotte.

'No hurdles, no stupid prancing . . . and those leg-breaking brick walls, no way. One scratch on this flank and it's goodbye Melrose.'

'What?'

'It's a cool street in Los Angeles where gals like me hang out.'

'I'm a good rider. You won't get hurt.'

The kid just didn't get it. 'I'll make you a deal. You call my producer Joel Gold, tell him where to find me, I'll get you a signed photo of Sarah-Jane Sweeney.'

'Who's she?' asked Charlotte.

'My point exactly. When I get out of here I'm switching to serious drama. I got this idea: Nelson Mandela as a filly . . . daring, good looking and above all, completely and utterly selfless. I wouldn't even have to act.'

'Okay. I'll call your producer as soon as we make the JOES.'

Leila snapped. 'What do you think I am? A charity? I'm an actor, kid. I don't help anybody, I *entertain*, get it? That's my gift to the world. It's much better than actually *helping*.'

Charlotte folded her arms defiantly. 'Now, you listen here . . .'

But then she pulled up, sensing something was different. She looked around to see The Evil Three staring at her as if she were a dead bug in the soup.

# Chapter 9

'Who were you talking to?' asked Emma accusingly.

Charlotte couldn't admit to talking to a horse. 'Um . . . myself.'

The others swapped the sort of looks that Charlotte's dad and the other stockmen swapped when they had to get into a pen with a mad bull.

'I heard two voices,' said Lucinda.

Rebecca was still half-deaf from last night's experiment with Emma's phone but, wanting to be useful, added, 'I saw her lips moving.'

'Two voices, one talking about acting or something.' Emma's look bored into Charlotte.

'And you're the only one in here,' said Lucinda weightily.

Charlotte was still trying to work out a plausible answer.

'Are you schizo?' asked Emma.

Rebecca said, 'She could be possessed by the devil.

In horror movies that always happens.'

Charlotte glared at her. Rebecca shrank back.

Lucinda sighed. 'Look, we just came to tell you that we think it would be better if you moved to another room. And if you're schizo, well, you know, you might need two beds anyway.'

The others nodded, as if this made sense. Charlotte was very angry now.

'I'm not schizo, okay?'

Emma shrugged. 'Well, there's only you and the horse. I guess she was the one talking?'

'Actually, she was.'

Charlotte regretted it as soon as it was out of her mouth but she couldn't stop now. 'I know it's pretty crazy. In fact, I thought it might have been you guys playing a trick on me. But it's her. She can speak like a human.' She turned to Leila. 'Go on, show them.'

Leila was horrified by this course of events. She regretted having spoken up to the rube. Loneliness, she guessed. Fortunately, this kid Charlie was seen as the local fruitcake anyway so all she had to do was keep quiet. Which she did.

Charlotte grew very angry.

'She's just doing this to annoy me. Come on, Leila, tell them about your new project.'

When Charlotte looked back, the other girls had

already backed away to the stable's entrance. Then they were gone.

'Now look what you've done,' she snapped at Leila.

Miss Strudworth straightened the bone china in the cabinet that had occupied this room since old Tobias' days. She was still a little wounded from that horrible caricature. She glanced across at the large photograph of her favourite royal, Princess Anne. You know what it's like, she thought. She had met the Princess once. In competition. That marvellous memory drew her gaze to the big glass case in the middle of the room where her wonderful pony, Zucchini, stared back at her through glassy eyes. It was ten years now since Zucchini had passed away. She'd had him stuffed and placed here so that she'd always have at least one companion. She moved over to the mantlepiece and dusted the trophies she had won as a young girl. First in dressage, first in jumps, first in cross-country. There had been a time when Miss Strudworth had hoped she might have had to scrunch up those trophies to fit the trophies of a husband on the shelf but, alas, it was not to be. Now at the age of forty-two, she had resigned herself to being purely and simply

Miss Strudworth, the very best equestrian mentor in the southern hemisphere.

A knock on the door derailed her train of thought.

'Enter.'

Three of the precocious princesses shuffled in. Strudworth wondered what on earth this would be about. A cable service not working? Poor reception on their mobile phones? No wood-fired pizza?

'Yes?' she enquired, raising an eyebrow that said *don't waste my time*.

The Evil Three brought Strudworth up-to-date with Charlotte's weird behaviour in the stables.

Rebecca was now going on about her brother and sister.

'I mean, they're in therapy but that's only because it's like . . . cool, you know? They're not actually mad.'

Strudworth pointed out that there was little evidence to suggest Charlotte Richards was mad.

'I do applaud you all for your heartfelt concern for a fellow student.'

'Yeah, great,' said Emma, 'but does that mean we get her out of our room? What if she attacks us or something?'

Strudworth said there was no reason to believe Charlotte was violent.

Lucinda had seen her father wield the threat of the law like an axe and now she demonstrated the family lineage. She said that if Strudworth was prepared to take that position in court, she supposed it was her call.

'But you know, if the unimaginable *did* happen and say we woke up and found she'd . . .'

'Plucked our eyebrows without permission.' Rebecca felt good about that addition.

'Right, or, you know, worse, taken a knife –' began Emma.

'And cut a hole in our Dolce and Gabbana outfits . . .' Lucinda suggested.

'But in a really *uncool* way,' added Rebecca, wanting to emphasise the point.

'Then the damages bill would be – oh, think of a seven-digit number?'

Lucinda smiled that killer smile of hers.

Strudworth felt the blood drain from her face. A settlement like that would cost her Thornton Downs. She barely met expenses as it was. What could she do? She couldn't lose the place. No, they really gave her no choice. Besides, Richards might be better off on her own.

Charlotte stared at her new room. Bare concrete walls and floors, if you didn't count the pipes that ran into the ceiling. No windows. And it was hot and stuffy from the boiler in the corner. Miss Strudworth pointed brightly at the fold-up camp bed.

'Quite cosy, really. You can use the bathroom on the second floor. And I'll get a clothes rack put outside for you.'

The room might be the pits but it was better than having to share with those witches. Charlotte put down her backpack, saying nothing. Strudworth coughed with embarrassment.

'But before you really settle in I'd like you to come and meet Mr Hatcher, the academy counsellor. He wants to know all about the, er, horse.'

❁ ❁ ❁

Mr Hatcher was a balding, pudgy man with glasses and a dirty bow-tie. His desk was cluttered with old coffee mugs and saucers with crumbs on them. It took up most of the small office, which was somewhere on the ground floor near the kitchen area. Hatcher rocked back on his big leather chair and looked over the notes in front of him. Every now and again he darted a lustful glance towards an open packet of chocolate biscuits but he resisted taking one, although he desperately wanted to hoe in.

Charlotte sat patiently on a small chair, wishing she were riding Stormy through the red desert. Seemingly satisfied with his notes, Hatcher looked up at Charlotte.

'So, Leila . . .'

'Charlotte. Leila's the horse.'

Hatcher was stunned at the response – and thrilled. This much so soon!

'Ah, I see,' he said to himself as he scrawled 'dual personality' on the pad in front of him. 'The *horse* is Leila and *you* are Charlotte.'

He leaned in close, hoping to penetrate the dissociative personality right off. But the girl simply stared at him. 'Can you tell me, Leila . . .'

'Charlotte,' replied Charlotte firmly.

'Just checking,' laughed Hatcher. 'Can you tell me what triggered this episode?'

He smirked at his clever pun. 'Trigger' was, of course, one of the most famous horses in the movies.

Charlotte was in a quandary. She didn't want to tell Mr Hatcher the truth because he would almost certainly not believe her, but her father and mother had said you must always tell the truth. So she told Mr Hatcher how she had asked Leila to help Charlie win a place in the JOES, and Leila had refused, saying she wouldn't because she was a famous Hollywood actor.

On his pad Hatcher scribbled 'delusions of grandeur'.

'And did Leila ever say why she wouldn't talk to anybody else?'

'Yes. She said she didn't want hypodermics jabbed into her butt and electrodes in her brain.'

Hatcher managed a forced laugh. 'Our profession doesn't do that any more.' He looked down at his notes again. 'I see your mother died four years ago?'

Charlotte nodded.

'How did you feel about that? Did you shut yourself away from the world?'

'No. I was sad but Dad said we had to go on, because that's what Mum wanted.'

Hatcher thought he saw it all now.

'And that was when you first met Leila, right?'

Charlotte shook her head. 'No, I told you, I only met her here.'

ɔ ɔ ɔ ɔ

Leila looked at the oats once more, hoping if she stared at them long enough they would turn into a Big Mac with fries. Nope. No matter how long she stared, it made no difference. Well, she couldn't wait any longer, she would have to find a phone and call Mr Gold.

Getting out of the stable was easy. But now she had the problem of sneaking across the open lawn to the big building where the phones would be. She looked left and right – the coast was clear. She trotted across the lawn and pushed open a fly-screen door. So far so good. She made her way into a big room that looked like an office of some sort. Good, a phone was on the desk. Even better, it was covered in stickers with numbers for Emergency and so on. One said 'International Operator'. Leila knocked the receiver off with her nose, picked up a pen in her teeth and used it to touch dial the number. A woman's voice answered.

'Country, please?'

'USA. I'm looking for a Mr Joel Gold of Hollywood, California.'

The woman asked Leila to hold a moment. Then she came back on.

'I'm sorry, that number is private. I can't give it out.'

Can't give it out!!!

'Listen, sister, do you have any idea who you're talking to –'

Clunk. She'd hung up on her! The nerve. Leila

thought hard. Whose number did she know that she could call to pass a message onto Joel? Of course. Her best friend, Hilary. Her number was easy to remember because it was the same as Leila's birthday with a five on the end. Leila dialled. The phone rang a few times and then picked up. Leila nearly screamed with excitement. She could just imagine Hilary sitting poolside.

'Hilary here.'

Oh. Now Leila saw the problem. Hilary didn't actually know Leila could talk, even though they'd hung out together heaps.

'Hel-lo?' Hilary was sounding impatient.

'Hi, Hils, you don't know me but I'm a friend of Leila.'

There was a pause. 'Who?'

'You know, Leila, that gorgeous horse you had up at your pool party last month.'

'Listen, honey, any friend of that freeloader is no friend of mine. At my last party she broke into the kitchen, scoffed every last canapé and barfed on my floor. When I went to get a mop to clean it up, or actually, to find the maid to tell her to clean it up, Leila jumped out at me in a *Scream* mask . . .'

Leila smiled, remembering her little joke.

'. . . so-o-o uncool.'

Leila felt a little shudder go through her. Hilary, her best pal, was calling her uncool?

Hilary continued, 'And as for her dancing, my maid was scrubbing horseshoe marks off my wall for a month. Goodbye.'

Clunk.

Leila was shattered, absolutely shattered. She'd always thought she had a real friend in Hilary. Well, no matter, she'd call . . . but try as she might, she couldn't think of anybody else to call.

Hatcher now stood in Strudworth's office reading from his notes.

'Charlotte has no female authority figure. She loves horses. What more simple way to create a belief system than a talking horse? Then if she fails at the academy, she can blame it all on the horse.'

Strudworth nodded thoughtfully.

'So it's the pressure?'

'Exactly.' Hatcher put his hand up to prop himself against a glass case and then realised he was staring at that creepy horse. He pulled his hand away and stood up straight. 'She's not insane, she's just . . . un-*stable* – get it?'

Strudworth didn't find his pun amusing. Especially not after he'd left greasy fingerprints all over the case of her stuffed Zucchini.

Hatcher continued. 'Essentially, she's a young girl looking for a lot of attention.'

'So for now?'

Hatcher was emphatic.

'Do nothing.' A little too emphatic – he felt the last of the chocolate biscuits working its way up from his stomach. He probably shouldn't have eaten the whole packet. 'Put the ball in her court.'

In the stables, The Evil Three were cleaning their tack within earshot of the depressed Leila. She had to find some way of getting out of this disgusting prison.

'Well, at least that's one less competitor for the JOES,' said Lucinda.

'That's something,' added Emma. 'I'm under so much pressure. Daddy's organised to telecast the parade of all riders and horses who make the JOES.'

Leila and Rebecca were thrilled. 'We'll be on TV?'

'Worldwide if you make it.'

Leila's ears suddenly pricked up. *A worldwide telecast?* Tommy or Mr Gold would be bound to see it.

Or somebody else who knew her would. Oh yes, this was her way home!!!

Then a cold, hard reality poked its nose in – to make the telecast, she and the rube would have to make the JOES.

ᴐ ᴐ ᴐ ᴐ

In the stuffy boiler room, Charlotte lay on her back and thought of home. How she wished she were there beneath blue skies, not a TV or mobile phone in sight. Just Stormy, Rusty and her dad. It was horrible here, worse than she had feared. Not one friend. She didn't belong here any more than that selfish Leila did. Just her luck to get some egotistical, movie-star, talking horse!!!

She reached across to her saddle and clutched the small plush toy horse she had attached. Then she went to sleep, dreaming of her mother's face.

# Chapter 10

The next morning Charlotte headed to the stables, trying to put out of her head the previous day's problems. Clearly Mr Hatcher thought she was loco but, as she could do nothing to dissuade him of that, there was no point worrying about it. In all likelihood her name had already been scratched off the JOES list. Part of her wanted to head straight back to Snake Hills – but how could she face all those people who had given up what little they had to send her here? Besides, she owed it to herself and the memory of her mum to do her best. As for that treacherous, conceited horse, Leila, well, if she wasn't going to speak, Charlotte could easily return the compliment.

Today, she was the first girl into the stables, figuring she'd need extra time to saddle up Leila. Prepared for battle, she walked down to the stall. She was astonished to find Leila standing alert and ready.

'What took you so long?' said Leila. 'I've been up since five.'

'I'm not talking to you,' Charlotte hissed back.

'Hey, sorry about yesterday but what could I do?'

Charlotte was miffed. 'Better they think I'm a freak than you?'

'Don't be like that. You'll see. I've turned over a new leaf.'

And to Charlotte's surprise she found that Leila was indeed compliant. In fact, she was quite perfect.

Leila was hating every second of this sucky behaviour but years in the movie industry had taught her that sometimes you just had to play the game. Despite all her good intentions, she still flinched when the saddle went on. It had some fluffy horse toy hanging off it. What was this? A nursery or a stable? Even though this uncool appendage offended her sense of style, Leila held her tongue. She caught the grey mare eyeing her suspiciously and threw a look back at her that said, 'You'll be eating my dirt before the day is out.'

ᗡ ᗡ ᗡ ᗡ

Miss Strudworth was surprised to see Charlotte Richards leading a well-behaved horse out of the stables. Well, at least that was a start. Mind you, she hadn't mounted yet. The girls fell into a straight line, their horses beside them. Strudworth blew her whistle and was gratified to see them all mount as one, even Richards.

'Proceed to the arena,' commanded Strudworth. 'We'll be practising sprint and stop today.'

Charlotte was elated when Leila trotted smartly to the arena. Strudworth began the exercise, blowing the whistle first to start at a gallop and then once more to signal a dead stop. Charlotte was surprised to find Leila was actually very good. Other horses overshot the mark but Leila stopped with precision.

The first couple of sprints Leila handled as easily as a spoon in a cold sundae. As a little filly her mother had forced her to take lots of classes. Not everything had been lost in her Hollywood indulgence. By the third sprint, however, she was starting to wheeze. Her legs were like jello. Boy, was she out of shape. Fortunately, the woman who looked like a horse called a halt to the exercise. The kid whispered in her ear, 'Well done, you're really good.' Like, she didn't know that? Not that Leila had the energy to argue. She was knackered and looking forward to a nice long nap. That was something else she was really good at. In fact she was starting to doze as she stood there with the horsy woman droning about something in the background.

'. . . and next, the hurdle.'

HURDLE!!!

Leila snapped wide awake. Jumps! She hissed out the side of her mouth, 'No way. I can't do this.'

Charlotte said quietly, 'Trust me.'

The first thing you ever learned in Hollywood was 'trust nobody'.

Charlotte said, 'You'll feel me give the signal with my knees. Just shut your eyes and imagine you're Tinkerbell in *Peter Pan*.'

Leila's heart was pounding. 'Tinkerbell, right.' She couldn't help but think of her father. They said he was the bravest horse with the biggest leap. He pulled all the hardest stunts. But in the end he jumped once too often and it killed him.

Strudworth looked over and nodded the command. 'Richards.'

Charlotte started Leila towards the hurdle. It wasn't high like a steeple. It was a pretty easy jump . . . for a trained horse. But how would somebody like Leila manage?

Leila charged towards the hurdle – ten metres, five metres – NO, she couldn't do this. She veered away.

Charlotte wheeled Leila back around. She was

aware of Strudworth seated on her horse nearby. Charlotte could just imagine what she was thinking: the Richards girl had started well today but now that things were getting tough, she couldn't cut the mustard. Charlotte wanted to prove her wrong but Leila was scared and there was no point yelling at her. She whispered, 'Listen, you have to trust me.'

Leila spoke up as best she could with the bridle in her mouth. 'I . . . on't . . . trust . . . y . . . own . . . mother.'

Charlotte had dealt with scared horses before. 'This isn't Hollywood. This is Neverland. And you're Tinkerbell. Understand?'

Charlotte now had Leila facing the hurdle. Leila could see the grey mare and the other horses sniggering off to the side. They really didn't think she could do it. In fact, she wasn't sure she could do it either, but hadn't she felt the same way about that walk-on part in *Buffy* that had made her career? She was Leila. She could do anything. She felt herself heading towards the hurdle. She could do it, sure she could.

But then a big black shadow called doubt swooped in – ten metres, five metres – with every stride the hurdle got bigger and bigger and the shadow darker and darker. She felt the kid's signal, closed her eyes. 'I'm Tink, I'm Tink . . .'

To Charlotte, everything went into slow motion. Leila's legs bent and pushed and then they left the earth and sailed through the air. Charlotte loved this moment, part-bird, part-horse, part-human. The hurdle passed beneath and the ground came up to meet them as they landed with a powerful thump.

Leila didn't believe she'd died but she couldn't be one hundred per cent sure. She still had her eyes closed. 'Can I open them now?'

She felt the kid pat her on the neck. 'Yes, you can open them.'

She did. And looked back at the hurdle. It didn't look so big any more. In fact it was puny. She felt the urge to dance.

'Well done,' said Charlotte.

They were out of earshot of anybody else. 'Othin to it. I made u look good.'

Charlotte smiled. 'You've changed your tune.'

Leila protested. 'I never scared. It's called acting.'

From the distance The Evil Three were watching and they were not happy. Rebecca summed it up. 'She's actually not bad.'

Competition for a place in the JOES had just got hotter.

ɔ ɔ ɔ ɔ

Feathers had been trying desperately to find some way of putting Mr Gold and Tommy onto the bad guy who'd led Leila astray with the pizza. He couldn't just start talking or then he'd become the subject of scientific experiment himself and he would never again see the open skies. No, he had to be clever about this. He had to do something to make them notice the suspicious guy and then get them to think it had all been their intuition or something.

After a couple of days he had hit upon the solution. First he had saved all his seed. That meant dieting like crazy, which wasn't so hard as he was already so upset he could barely eat. Seed came in little husks that were dark on one side and light on the other. Often, just for the fun of it, Feathers would make patterns out of this light and dark.

Over the last two days, seed by seed, he'd taken that creativity a step further. Using his tray as a frame, out of the seed he had constructed a black and white identikit of the crim he had seen stalking around the night Leila went missing. Above it he had written 'Gilty'. He figured if he could get Tommy and Mr Gold to notice his handiwork, the message and the image might crawl into their subconscious. Then, the next time they saw the crim hanging around, they might pay more attention to him. Feathers just needed the right opportunity to get them to see his artwork.

And now it was presenting itself. Tommy and Joel Gold were in the trailer talking about Leila. Tommy had just told Mr Gold that the latest Leila replacement, the fifth they'd tried, was no good.

Joel Gold shook his head sadly. 'You're right. There's only one Leila.'

They were standing right in front of the cage. Feathers knew this was his best chance. Using all his strength, he lifted his tray with his beak. Gradually the sketch rose up so that now it was right between their profiles. They were looking at each other but if they turned, they would see it.

Gold said, 'If only we had a lead on the nag-nappers we could give the police.'

Tommy shook his head. 'Somebody must have seen something.'

Feathers reached up with his wing and brushed his bell so it tinkled. He felt Joel Gold turning towards him. YES!!!

Joel Gold turned to face the cage but right then something tickled his nose. Probably seed – he was allergic to it, always had been. He had no time to cover his mouth as he let out an enormous sneeze, blowing Feathers' artwork to the four corners of the trailer.

'Bless you,' said Tommy, offering a tissue.

Neither of them noticed Feathers banging his head into the bars in frustration – all his hard work had been turned to dust.

ↄ ↄ ↄ ↄ

The night of her hurdles effort Leila stood tall in her stall, grinning across at the grey mare. 'So what did you think of that, grandma?'

The mare muttered something inaudible and turned her back. Typical, thought Leila. Just like in tinsel-town. People couldn't handle her success. Well, she'd be back there soon with a hot body and a whole new bag of tricks. The rube was a pain in the fetlock but Leila could handle her easy enough. Looking on her as a kind of cheap personal trainer was probably best. Things weren't turning out so bad after all.

ↄ ↄ ↄ ↄ

That was a sentiment shared by Charlotte. She sat alone in the dining room, feeling the eyes of The Evil Three upon her but, rather than being concerned, she was pleased to have them on edge. She ate with great relish. Leila had proved she could be a pretty talented equestrian horse and now that she had realised her attitude had been all wrong, they could make a top team.

That night, for the first time since she'd been at Thornton Downs, Charlotte lay in bed in her small, stuffy boiler room and felt content. It didn't really matter how the other girls treated her. It didn't really matter if Mr Hatcher and Miss Strudworth thought she was delusional. In Leila she had a real friend now. Together they could make the JOES. She shut her eyes and went to sleep instantly, with a wide smile on her face.

Next morning Charlotte burst brightly into the stables. 'Hi there, Leila, how did you sleep?'

Leila moaned. She had barely slept at all. Every joint in her body ached. When they were out in the open heading towards the arena and able to speak privately, Leila announced she was worried she had typhoid fever.

Charlotte felt her. 'No temperature.'

'Maybe it's one of those no-temperature diseases. Every muscle in my body feels like it's been stitched.'

'That's just good old-fashioned soreness. You exercised muscles you've probably never used before. Once we get warmed up you'll be fine.'

Leila didn't believe her but by the time they got to the arena she was feeling a whole lot better.

Strudworth was in the centre of the ring. A row of flags on small stands stretched from one side to the other.

'Today it's slalom practice,' Strudworth announced. 'The object is to move between all the flags without touching them.' Strudworth demonstrated on her horse. Charlotte was impressed. For someone who looked so awkward on her own feet, Strudworth on a horse was fluid, balanced and precise.

Leila stifled a yawn. Easy peasy. One of her films, *On Thin Ice*, had featured Sarah-Jane as an aspiring ice-polo player and Leila and Sarah had spent a week of intensive training doing this very same slalom stuff on an ice-field. Well, Leila had feigned a cold and the stunt horse had had to do it, but all the same, really. Leila had watched the stunt horse doing it from her cosy caravan while drinking large mugs of hot chocolate. Nothing to it.

'Follow my lead,' said Charlotte. 'You'll be fine.'

Sure, sure. Leila began confidently enough but then it was Whack! Whack! Whack! One flag after another slapping her nose or her butt. Obviously they had cheated and made the gaps too narrow.

Charlotte hissed down at her. 'You can't do this by yourself. Let me help.'

Leila ignored her. Whack! Whack! Whack!

'If you don't listen to me, we'll keep doing it till you do.'

'Okay, okay. You show me how much better you can do.'

And to Leila's surprise she did. When she followed Charlotte's commands they only hit one more flag. By the time they came back on the reverse run, Leila knew where Charlotte was going to send her and they did the slalom not just quickly and without error but with style, as if Leila was stepping out on the dancefloor of one of those Sunset Boulevard discos. Come to think of it, this could be a brand new little dance she could show Hilary, Paris and those other gals. Oh, they were just gonna love having her back.

ↄ ↄ ↄ

That night Charlotte didn't go to dinner. The last thing she wanted was the company of other girls. Instead she picked up some bread rolls from the kitchen en route to the stables, which were deserted except for the horses.

Leila was excited to see her.

'Hey, girlfriend! I've been reminding these nags here how we kicked their butt today.'

The grey mare, which Emma had selected as her mount, lifted her lip into a sneer. Leila's eyes bugged out at the rolls.

'*Fresh bread!*'

Charlotte rubbed Leila's muzzle and fed her one.

'Not that fresh.'

Leila woofed one down almost whole. 'Hey, compared to the chaff I've been on here, this is caviar.'

'I have to say, I was wrong about you, Leila. I thought you were bone lazy but I couldn't have asked for a better effort these last couple of days.'

Leila couldn't care less what she thought of her so long as she kept the bread rolls coming.

'People take a little time to get to know the real me.'

The grey mare rolled her eyes. Leila gave her the mind-your-own-business stare. The kid began brushing her. This was more like it. Hanging out here for a few weeks wouldn't be too foul at all if only some pizza could be thrown in. She tossed the idea to her new best buddy, Charlie.

'Pizza? No way. You still need to lose weight.'

'How about a little ice-cream sundae, chocolate and caramel topping, nuts . . .'

'No.'

'What if we hold on the nuts?'

'No, we have a big challenge ahead of us.'

Leila decided not to push it. Things had a way of panning out. She looked over and noticed the saddle on the stall. The twee velvet horse dangled annoyingly. What if she was seen wearing that on worldwide TV? She'd be the laughing stock of the Viper Room. She had a reputation to uphold. Leila jutted her jaw at the toy.

'Any chance we could lose Poco here?'

'No way. My mum made it.'

Leila felt a twinge of envy. Imagine a mom who actually made you something? Even something as appallingly corny as this. Leila's mom had never made her anything except angry. When Leila was younger her mom always returned from her latest overseas tour with some stupid little doll or something. Like that was supposed to make everything right. These days she didn't bother, she'd got the message.

To keep the kid brushing, Leila figured she should start some conversation.

'So your mom is pretty proud of you, I guess.'

'She died. Not long after she made that horse.'

Leila felt awful. A real hoof-in-the-mouth job.

'I'm sorry, Charlie. Bum deal.'

The kid just said, 'Yeah,' and kept brushing.

Leila didn't know what to say. For a long time there was no sound except the rhythm of the brush. She decided to take another stab.

'So, tell me about this place you're from?'

The kid did. For well over an hour. Leila found herself doing something she rarely had before – listening. It was actually pretty interesting in a weird way, though the place sounded like Tijuana without the people. Imagine no cable and no macchiato? Leila perked up when Charlie got onto mustering. Could come in handy if Tommy ever did a western or cattle ranch movie.

The best stuff, though, was the stuff about the kid's folks. How Charlie and her mom and dad used to pile into the car and drive, like, two hours to find a shady spot where Charlie's mom would spread a picnic blanket, hopefully not on a bull ants' nest, and they would sit and eat boiled eggs and cucumber and pretend they were by a lake watching ducks.

Leila expected Charlie to be sad when she told those stories but she was bright as a button reliving those good times. Leila got a pang wishing she'd driven somewhere with her folks and eaten boiled eggs and cucumber. Sure, she'd been to lots of opening night Hollywood shindigs with sushi, chicken yakitori, canapés, live salsa bands and free slushies, but when she started telling the kid about Hollywood and how great those parties were, she had to force her smile. She didn't quite feel it in her heart like Charlie obviously did.

Eventually Charlotte thought to check her watch. She was shocked to find it was well after nine p.m. She had to go. Leila couldn't believe three hours had passed. It felt it had gone a lot quicker than *Lord of the Rings*.

'I'll see you tomorrow.'

Charlotte kissed Leila on the muzzle. It was a different sort of kiss to what you got at the restaurant of the Four Seasons. They were air-kisses, missing the cheek by a mile. Usually Leila would snarl if somebody tried this sort of smooch. She didn't like people getting close to her. But tonight she let it go. After all, she needed to make the JOES so she supposed she should put up with it, keep the kid happy.

꒩ ꒩ ꒩ ꒩

The next week breezed by. Charlotte spent practically every spare minute with Leila. When they weren't improving their dressage work on the arena, stepping between rubber tyres, hurdling, spinning and reversing, they were swapping tales of home. Leila had so many fantastic stories about the movies she'd been in. Of course, Charlotte had no idea who these famous actors were but now and again she would sneak a look at the magazines the other girls brought down to meals and she'd realise that the actors on the cover were Leila's Hollywood friends.

Leila was gradually getting fitter. From being the worst of the pairings at Thornton, Leila and Charlotte were closing in on the very best, who Charlotte grudgingly conceded included The Evil Three.

Charlotte and Leila had got into the habit of taking long afternoon rides to the farthest corner of the property, where they could natter freely away from prying ears. Ninety per cent of what Leila talked about was food. What this or that actor turned on for their 'opening' or engagement or break-off-of-engagement parties. Whenever Charlotte tried to get Leila to talk about her mum she muttered 'show pony' and changed the subject. Today, though, she had opened up about her father.

'He made over thirty movies. He kept doing more and more dangerous stunts to help provide for me and Mom. All that time, not once did the studio take him to a classy restaurant. Chaff every day of his life until he died. And they buried him where he fell. That's the studios for you.'

'And you hate them for it.'

'Of course I do.'

'And your mum?'

Leila got defensive. 'I was a kid. She should have been there.'

'She was being a mum and dad for you.'

'Well, she failed. Hey, did I ever tell you about the time J-Lo and I caught the bus?'

Charlotte was aware Leila was changing the subject. She couldn't imagine anybody who had a mother not wanting to spend all the time they had with them. They were cantering along the top of a wooded ridge, the sun orange and fat and beginning to sink, as if it had just finished a long lunch and wanted a snooze. Leila finished her J-Lo story. Charlotte felt she'd missed something.

'I don't get it. You caught a bus, went one stop and got off.'

'Yeah.'

Leila was smirking and shaking her head at the memory.

'But what was the big deal?'

'We rode the bus – that was the big deal. Hey, did I ever tell you about the time in Rome? The studio had this amazing cake made in the shape of a Ferrari . . .'

'What's that?'

Charlotte had spotted something moving in the valley below.

Leila didn't miss a beat. 'A Ferrari is an Italian racing car . . .'

'No . . . *that!*'

Charlotte pointed below where she had seen movement. Through the trees they could make out a familiar shape.

'That, my friend, is a horse,' said Leila smugly.

Charlotte decided they had better investigate and sent Leila forward down the hill. It became very slippery near the bottom and she needed all her skill to keep Leila from sliding, though Leila, of course, would have claimed it was only her experience working on some dance film clip that kept them upright.

Finally they came to the floor of the valley. Fifty metres away a big black horse looked over at them.

'He's magnificent,' said Charlotte as they trotted towards him.

Leila wasn't excited. Any horse that good looking just had to be a gelding. As she got closer she noticed something familiar about him. The way he stood, the way he looked over like he was so cool . . .

*Wait a second.*

She knew this horse. This was bully-boy from the paddock back near the film lot! She heard Charlotte's sharp intake of breath.

'Over there.'

Bully-boy was forgotten as Charlotte reefed her around. Now she saw it. A bundle on the ground, twenty metres away. The bundle moved. It was a boy, about Charlie's age, and he was trying to get to his feet.

'Are you okay?'

Charlotte dismounted and began running in one fluid movement. The boy blinked and looked up, a little dazed. His helmet was lying off to the side.

'Thanks, I'm fine.'

'You don't look fine.' Charlotte could see he was having trouble standing.

'No, I guess I'm not a hundred per cent. Warrior slipped coming down the hill and I fell off. No damage to the head, that's too thick, but I think I twisted my ankle.'

Charlotte could easily have disagreed about the head part. His head looked fine to her, actually pretty darn cute if you liked that sort of thing in boys. Not that Charlotte did. His assessment of his ankle seemed on the money. He was trying to hop on his good leg.

'What are you doing here?' he asked casually, picking up his helmet.

'What are *you* doing here, you mean. This is Thornton Downs.'

He grinned.

'Your geography's not too hot. You're on Milthorp land.'

He must have seen the doubtful look on her face.

'Did you cross the stream about two ks back?'

She confirmed she had.

'That's the border.'

Charlotte felt immediately foolish. And then worried. What if Strudworth found out? There was bound to be some rule against it.

'You won't tell, will you?'

He laughed out loud. 'No way. I don't want everybody to know I was dumb enough to fall off my horse.'

Charlotte liked him immediately for saying that. None of the girls at Thornton Downs would ever have admitted messing up. They were all too busy trying to psych each other out.

'Would you mind?'

He nodded at the horse and for a moment Charlotte didn't understand what he meant. Then she realised he needed help to get on.

'You're not going to try and ride with that ankle. You can't even walk.'

'I'll be fine once I'm on.'

Leila only half heard this interchange. She was too busy circling the bully-boy stallion.

'So, we meet again,' he whinnied.

Leila snarled back in horse. 'Yeah, we meet and we say goodbye.'

'Suits me.'

'Me too.'

They continued to eye each other warily as Charlotte helped the boy over. Leila thought the boy wasn't bad looking in a boy band sort of way. Charlie could do worse.

Charlotte watched the boy get his bad foot into the stirrup.

'I won't be able to put any pressure on it, so if you could just steady Warrior . . .'

She did and the boy pulled himself back into the saddle. She saw him wince but he settled in and picked the reins back up.

'Thanks, see you round.'

He trotted off, struggling to stay straight. Charlotte felt Leila's hot breath on her neck.

'Hope he's better than his ride.'

Charlotte was surprised at Leila's negativity.

'I thought Warrior looked impressive.'

'Hey, Warrior thinks Warrior's impressive. What's the story with the spunk?'

'The spunk?'

'The boy. Come on, you can't tell me you didn't notice he was cute.'

'I didn't notice.'

It was a white lie. Charlotte had noticed but it wasn't like that impressed her. She was more impressed by his owning up to being a klutz and falling off his horse.

'Sure you didn't notice. What's his name?'

It was only then that Charlotte realised she had no idea. Not that it mattered. She would probably never see him again.

By the time they got back to the stables, Charlotte had been regaled at length with Leila's previous encounter with Warrior. Charlotte tried to point out that from what Leila had told her, she hadn't exactly been friendly to the other horses, but Leila failed to see it. She was a star, they should have been happy just to share a paddock with her. Leila finally let go of her outrage to bring the subject back to treats.

'Come on, Charlie, just a little itty-bitty sundae with whipped cream.'

As always, Charlotte patiently explained that they still had a long way to go. Leila replied that was what Charlotte had said a week ago and since then Leila hadn't put a hoof wrong.

'The trials are just three days away. You can last,' said Charlotte firmly. She put away the brush, kissed Leila on the forehead and left. Leila watched her exit through narrowing eyes. She liked the kid, she really did, but fair was fair. If she wanted a treat, she would get a treat. One little treat, what harm could that do? There was more than one way to scoop a sundae. She had tried being polite and asking for the kid's help but the fact was, she didn't need it. She could do it all by her little ol' self.

つ つ つ

The dining room was alive with the sound of girls gossiping. Strudworth had announced they were to assemble there for some special announcement and each girl in the room had her own ideas as to what that might be. Well, each except for Charlotte. She didn't really care and had no desire to find out. She had Leila. One good friend was all you ever needed.

When Strudworth entered the room and rapped her boots with her riding crop, the whole room fell into an excited silence.

'Tomorrow we have a special treat. A friendly jump-off against the boys from Milthorp.'

There was a collective intake of breath. Much to Charlotte's disgust, one girl – Charlotte had a feeling it may have been Rebecca – actually squealed.

Strudworth continued. 'We beat them last year but it will be a lot tougher this year because Todd Greycroft will be riding for them. So tally-ho, let's show those Milthorp boys what the gals from Thornton have.'

Some of the more enthusiastic girls started the Thornton chant.

'Thornton, Thornton the academy. We're the best as you will see. Point-to-point, hurdle, steeple, you can't touch the Thornton people. Gooooooo Thornton!!!'

In the stable Leila was dimly aware of some loud chanting in the background but she was primarily focused on the delectable pizza she was chomping. Overall she thought the Supremo was the best and she was glad she had ordered two. But the two Mexicanas were tasty and the Three Cheeses with thick crust also had something to recommend it. She smiled at how simple it had been. After all, she'd done all the hard work before when she'd tried to call Joel Gold.

She'd trotted out of the stables back to the office, dialled the pizza place whose menu was by the phone and ordered, emphasising they remember the bonus Cokes and sundaes. She'd spied the tin marked 'petty cash' by the phone. If they were going to call it 'petty' she guessed that meant nobody would miss it. She'd given Charlotte's name, told them she'd leave the cash with the horse Leila at the stables and to leave the pizzas there in case Charlotte was busy. Simple. The delivery guy had brought the pizzas right to her stall. Mmm, that pizza tasted fine. She let out a loud burp. Boy, that Mexicana was hot! She tried to get to her feet but it was struggle. Maybe she should have skipped the Three Cheeses?

The next day, Charlotte watched from the sidelines as Lucinda sent her horse over the last jump for a perfect round. She might not like her, but Charlotte had to admit she could certainly ride. The Thornton girls were lined up on one side of the arena, the Milthorp boys on the other. Both the boys and girls politely applauded each competitor. Thornton had done exceedingly well and was far enough ahead that now only a complete disaster would rob them of victory. Being the last to ride for Thornton, Charlotte was nervous but still confident. Leila had handled most of these manoeuvres very well just twenty-four hours earlier. Strudworth rode down the Thornton line like a general urging on her troops.

'Now, let's see what this Greycroft has got.'

All eyes, including Charlotte's, turned towards the Milthorp line. A magnificent, powerful black stallion eased out and moved to the arena. He looked awfully familiar. And so did the rider. It was the boy she had met the day before. *That* was Todd Greycroft! Knowing how badly he had twisted his ankle, Charlotte didn't think he'd have any chance of completing his round but to look at him you would never know there was anything wrong. He rode with a real fluidity.

She heard Rebecca gasp, 'He's gorgeous.'

Charlotte didn't think any boys were 'gorgeous'. A chocolate cream cake was gorgeous, not a boy. But he certainly could ride gracefully.

Leila narrowed her eyes at the sight of that bully-boy stallion trotting out into the arena as if he was Lord Muck. Huh! Leila hoped he broke a leg. But the way he sailed over jump after jump told her that wasn't likely. What a show-off!

Charlotte watched Todd Greycroft's round, riveted. She had always refused to believe that any boy could ride better than her but Todd Greycroft was very, very good. He finished his perfect round, doffed his helmet without conceit and moved back to the line. She suddenly felt a lump in her throat. Now it was up to her to make sure Thornton won.

'Richards,' commanded Strudworth.

Charlotte led Leila around to approach the low hedge. Both were confident and Leila sailed over it easily. On her return Leila made sure she made eye contact with the stallion. Her look said it all: 'That's right, buster, white girls can jump!' She felt Charlie turn her towards the hurdle and begin the approach.

All of a sudden things started getting blurry. It felt like she had a beach ball in her stomach. Too late, she realised she should never have had that second Mexicana. She tried to urge her fat, overstuffed body up into the air.

On the takeoff, Charlotte could feel that all was not right with Leila. Then she heard the dreaded 'clunk' of the hurdle pole rattling off behind. She saw

Strudworth's face fall while Lucinda's, Rebecca's and Emma's broke into smiles. It was galling but it would all be forgotten. Thornton was still well in front. The water jump was a cinch. SPLASH!

Leila's hooves wobbled in the mud. The smiles of The Evil Three grew bigger.

'What is your problem?' asked Charlotte angrily. They were far enough away not to be overheard.

'I'm sorry, I think I've got a virus,' said Leila.

Charlotte felt bad for snapping at her. She was much more worried about Leila than winning some silly event, though it was still uncomfortable to feel the eyes of everybody burning into her. Todd Greycroft would be watching and he'd think she was an absolute dud if she didn't clear the wall. Surely they could do it. She tried to gee herself up but as soon as they faced it she felt Leila sag. Trying to boost Leila's confidence, she said, 'Remember, those bricks are only cardboard.'

So is a pizza box and look at all the problems that caused, thought Leila.

Charlotte started her approach. She prayed it was going to be okay. Just one good jump and then she could get Leila back to her box and look after her. But as they got near the takeoff point Leila not only stopped but sank to her belly.

'Now that's what I call a refusal,' commented an excited Emma to Lucinda and Rebecca. Then, realising that Strudworth was looking their way, she quickly changed her broad grin into a false frown.

Todd Greycroft recognised the girl and horse he'd met the day before. He felt very sorry for her. He could tell there was something the matter with her horse.

When it stopped and lay down, the line of Milthorp boys cheered. Todd turned angrily towards them.

'What are you cheering for? They would have beaten us except for that horse.'

When she heard the cheering Charlotte felt humiliated. She wished she could turn invisible. No such luck. She would just have to bear it. There were worse things in life than a little humiliation. The most important thing was that Leila got better.

'It's okay, Leila, don't worry. You did your best. We'll get the vet to look at you.'

Leila fought to keep down a burp.

'No, no, I'm sure it's only temporary. In fact, I feel a little better already.' From the corner of her eye she caught the grey mare looking at her with barely concealed contempt. She shot back a look of her own. Big deal, so she didn't make the jump. She'd get over it next time. This was just a friendly. This didn't count.

Charlotte avoided the other girls on the way back to the stables. She was quite aware they blamed her for losing the jump-off but there was nothing she could do about that. She and Leila had done their best.

When they were alone in the stables Leila assured Charlotte she was already feeling much better and there was no need for a vet. Charlotte kissed her and told her not to worry about the jumps. The most important thing was to get better. She had wanted to stay but Leila insisted she would be fine with a little rest so Charlotte had reluctantly left her alone.

As she stepped outside, she got the shock of her life. Todd Greycroft was standing there.

'Hi. Charlotte, right?'

Charlotte was completely taken aback. 'Are you allowed to be here?'

'Probably not,' he shrugged. 'But I wanted to see how your horse was.'

'I think she's going to be fine.'

'And you, of course. That was rotten luck.'

Charlotte felt herself blushing. It was just too awful to think he'd seen that ride. 'I lost us the event,' she said bluntly.

'Nonsense. Your horse got sick. Could happen to any of us.'

It was nice of him to say so, even if she still felt guilty about it. 'You rode brilliantly,' she said. 'Bad ankle and all.'

He smiled. 'Thanks. When my ankle's better and your horse is well, we might have to race one another, don't you think? Loser can give the winner a Mars Bar.'

Charlotte grinned. 'That's an excellent idea.'

Todd looked around him to make sure he hadn't been spied. 'I had better be off. See you again, Charlotte.'

And before she could find the words to reply he was hopping off on one leg. He looked funny. But not silly. Boys like Todd never really looked silly.

Charlotte suddenly felt a whole lot better. Now she had two friends out here. She was almost floating as she made her way to the dining room but she came back down to earth when The Evil Three sidled up beside her.

'Nice jumping,' said Emma and the other two laughed. Charlotte fought the urge to pop somebody on the nose. She ate quickly by herself then returned to the boiler room, where she began writing a letter to her dad. This was the second time she had written and, like last time, she didn't come anywhere near telling him the truth. She wrote about the wonderful view from her room, the terrific food, and the great friend she had made, Leila. She didn't mention that Leila was a horse. There was a knock on her door and a girl named Caitlin poked her head in to tell her she was wanted in Strudworth's office immediately. Charlotte's first thought was that Strudworth was going to blast her for losing the jump-off. Then she panicked that something bad had happened with Leila's virus. She raced there as quickly as possible and knocked on the door.

'Come in, Richards, and close the door behind you.'

Charlotte did. She could tell that Miss Strudworth was upset about something.

'Is Leila all right?'

'Leila's fine. Can you explain what this was doing in her stall?'

Strudworth flashed a tin on which was written 'petty cash'.

Charlotte shook her head.

'You didn't take it from the downstairs office?'

'No.'

'Bevans found it in Leila's stall, hidden at the back. He also found a number of empty pizza cartons outside Leila's window. I made some enquiries with the pizza restaurant. They told me that Charlotte Richards ordered the pizzas and said that there would be cash left for them in the stall.'

Charlotte was angry. She knew exactly what had happened.

'Do you think I would be that stupid? It's quite obvious that Emma Cross and her friends are trying to set me up.'

Strudworth studied the girl in front of her. What she said was not beyond the realms of possibility.

'That's a very serious accusation,' she said.

'So is being told you're a thief.' Charlotte folded her arms defiantly.

# Chapter 11

A short time later The Evil Three stood before Strudworth in her office. Charlotte had been told to stand at the back. Strudworth wasted no time. She asked outright if they'd ordered pizzas in Charlotte's name. Rebecca was outraged.

'No way would I do that. Do you know how many calories there are in pizza?'

Strudworth looked to Emma and Lucinda. Lucinda acidly reminded Strudworth that her father was a successful defamation lawyer and wondered what Strudworth would do without the academy, the horses or the clothes on her back.

'What time did the call come through?' asked Emma.

Strudworth checked her notes.

'Six-twenty.'

Emma smiled smugly. 'Then it couldn't have been us because we were in the common room in front of a dozen students performing our Best Of *Charmed* routine.'

The others joined in the triumph.

'In fact,' added Lucinda, 'the only person who wasn't there was her.'

She nodded at Charlotte, who again felt the pressure had shifted back onto her. 'I was in my room, alone,' said Charlotte, and hated the fact that it sounded like an admission.

Strudworth sighed deeply. 'Very well. I'll need to think on this. Return to your rooms, please.'

As Charlotte left she felt Miss Strudworth's eyes on her back.

ᑐ ᑐ ᑐ ᑐ

'She thinks I did it!' Charlotte paced in the stable, explaining to Leila. 'I was so sure it was them. Did you see anybody near your stall?'

Leila hadn't foreseen this complication.

'Me? No, um, can't say I did.'

Charlotte started to work out the logic.

'Which means it must have been done while we were out, but then the order was taken at six-twenty.'

Slowly out of the fog of conjecture a solid picture

began to emerge, one she kicked herself for not seeing right off.

'Wait a second . . .' The image that had solidified in her mind was Leila the pizza-freak eating herself sick. 'Oh, how stupid have I been? It was you!'

Leila put on her most contrite voice.

'The tin said *petty* cash so I thought, who cares? If they call it petty it means it's insignificant, right? I just got a wicked taste for pizza.'

Charlotte was as angry as she had ever been. And deeply hurt. The only thing that had made Thornton Downs bearable had been her one good friend, Leila. But that friendship was worth nothing. Leila had just been using her.

'Sorry, kid. I didn't mean to cause trouble.'

Charlotte turned on Leila, fighting back tears.

'No, that's just it, you're not sorry at all. You don't care what happens to anybody but yourself.' She was seeing it all so clearly now. 'And that's why you were so poor over the jumps, wasn't it? You ate yourself sick. You're a truly selfish beast.'

'Hey, if I was that selfish I wouldn't have kept two slices of the Three Cheeses for you. I waited a whole extra hour, almost, before I ate them.'

'You aren't a real friend. You just wanted me to make the JOES so I would call your producer. Well, you can find some other bozo. I'm fed up with selfish, mean people – and horses. If this is what the JOES is all about then I don't want to be part of it.'

Oh, oh. Leila could see the palms of Hollywood receding fast. She tried to remember a script where she'd had to talk Sarah-Jane around.

'Charlie, Charlie, this is an overreaction.'

But Charlotte had made up her mind. She pulled her saddle from the stall.

'I hope you make it back to Hollywood, I really do. Then at least you'll be twenty thousand kilometres away.'

Leila watched her stomp up towards the stable exit. She couldn't let Charlotte have the last say.

'You've got a lot to learn, Charlie. You have a look at how actors react when they miss out on an Oscar. They don't storm out, they act dignified. It's only later they throw tantrums.'

But by now she was speaking to herself.

Leila snorted. The kid was bluffing. Where was she going to go?

ↄ ↄ ↄ ↄ

Nobody saw the small figure making its way through the grounds in the direction of the highway lugging the saddle. Charlotte fought the urge to cry. The JOES had been everything she had aspired to. She had wanted to make her dad proud. She had wanted to be graceful and beautiful like her mum. But it wasn't going to happen and the sooner she faced that the better.

She'd been kidding herself. To make the JOES you needed rich parents and lots of skills on how to be sneaky and bitchy that she'd never learned and had no intention of learning. She would go back to Snake Hills and be a stockman like her father. Next year she would win the Golden Buckle. She felt guilty about the people at Snake Hills who had put in money for her but she resolved to work hard and pay them back every cent. Better they put the money to good use than waste it. Strudworth was going to boot her out anyway. She figured she had just enough money for a bus fare to the city and a train fare from there to Snake Hills. She had never been to a big city before but she reckoned she could handle that. Nothing could be more unfriendly than here.

Leila did not sleep at all. She felt really bad. It wasn't just her tummy, either. In fact her tummy was nothing compared to how she felt in her heart.

'You ought to be ashamed of yourself,' the grey mare had whinnied after the kid had stormed off. Leila didn't need to be told. The shame she felt was a whole new emotion. She couldn't think of one other time in her whole life when she'd actually felt bad about making somebody else's life a misery. She'd never once worried about Sarah-Jane. With good reason – Sarah-Jane was a little witch who dug the heels of her riding boots into her. But maybe, Leila speculated, if she had been nicer to Sarah-Jane instead of competing with her, things might have been different?

And look at Tommy Tempest. He'd always treated Leila well but plenty of times Leila had made Tommy's life a misery just for the sport of it. And her mom, well, okay, maybe there was something in what Charlotte had said about her having to be a mom and a dad. Hopefully when Charlotte came around in the morning she wouldn't be quite so mad. Leila would promise not to even think about pizza until the end of the trials, and she would keep that promise. Leila looked out of her stall at the black night and prayed for dawn to hurry up.

ɔ ɔ ɔ ɔ

Somebody else who had slept fitfully that night was Miss Strudworth. Normally her hair net would be undisturbed when she awoke but this wretched business with the Richards girl had quite undone her. What was she to do? The evidence against her was compelling but not definitive. Expulsion was drastic. Thornton had never had a student expelled in its history. But on the other hand, theft was a most heinous crime that showed total lack of character. And the Richards girl had accused those others. No angels – certainly not, little witches in fact – but to smear somebody's character . . .

Oh dear, it was all so difficult. Strudworth really identified with the poor Queen and what it must be like to head *that* particular family. Strudworth had been in such a state that she had not even time for her toast and marmalade. She'd skipped breakfast and now sat on her horse, watching the girls fall into line.

Robotically, she reminded them that this was their last day of practice. 'Tomorrow we start your finals with dressage. Tuesday will be show-jumping and Wednesday we'll be finishing with the point-to-point.'

Something was not right and now she realised what it was. The face she most needed to see was not there.

'Has anybody seen Richards?'

Lucinda piped up.

'She wasn't at breakfast.'

Strudworth tried to keep the lid on her exasperation. 'Why didn't you tell me?'

Rebecca explained she had been listening to her iPod.

'And it's not like she's that noticeable,' added Emma, to general agreement.

Lucinda felt the need to elaborate. 'Her wardrobe is the pits.'

⊃ ⊃ ⊃
⊃ ⊂

A short time later a concerned Strudworth stood in the stables with Hatcher. They had checked the boiler room and found it cleaned out.

'Looks like Charlotte has run away.'

Leila listened to this development with dread building in her heart.

Hatcher sighed wearily, 'I guess she couldn't handle being caught. She's probably got a bus to the city and from there she'll get a coach or train back home.'

The idea of a thirteen-year-old country girl alone in the city troubled Strudworth greatly. There were too many dangers. She announced she would phone the police. She and Hatcher left.

Leila looked over at the condemnatory face of the grey mare.

'I know. I know,' she blurted.

A big city was tough enough for anybody to handle, but Charlie there! That would be like a little woolly lamb being led to the slaughter. The kid had no survival skills. There were bad people in the city, and Leila wasn't just thinking of agents and reviewers. She couldn't rely on police to find Charlotte. After all, Leila had been nag-napped, taken to the other side of the world, and no police had any idea where she'd gone. No, she was going to have to do it herself.

꒳ ꒳ ꒳

A few minutes later, Leila had snuck out of the barn, jumped four fences and made it through the bush and onto the highway. Inside the bus shelter she smelled baby powder. Odds on Charlie had been there as recently as this morning. Probably the buses didn't run in the evening and she'd had to spend the night on the bench here. Leila had no idea where the city was but given the air here was smog-free she guessed it wasn't anywhere close by. Oh well, looks like it was shanks's pony for now. She trotted off down the road.

About half an hour later she caught a break. Parked at a service station was a large truck carrying an empty swimming pool. Fortunately, with her recent practice, it was easy for Leila to jump up into the pool.

After about five minutes the driver came out of the shop carrying a hamburger. He didn't notice Leila as he bent to open his door.

'You heading for the city?' she called out, then ducked her head.

'Yeah,' the driver answered. He looked around to see who'd asked. There was no sign of anybody. He shook his head, mumbled that he'd have to stop doing these long hauls because they were making him nuts, then he climbed into his cab and turned on the engine.

⊃ ⊃ ⊃ ⊃

Sleeping in the bus shelter didn't present any real hardship to Charlotte. She'd slept on much rougher ground with fire ants nipping at her feet. The city, on the other hand, was so much noisier, smellier and scarier than she'd ever imagined. The buildings were so tall. She stepped onto the road to get a better look and a car-horn blared so loudly she nearly jumped out of her skin. With her heart pounding, she dived back onto the footpath. The driver of a van shouted at her as he roared past.

It was really strange here. There were so many people but nobody looked at anyone else, they all seemed to be too busy. Charlotte realised that Strudworth might have told the police about her so she kept out of the way of any policemen she saw. The bus driver had pointed out the train station, which she was relieved to see was only a few blocks from where she had been dropped. But it took a long time getting through the traffic.

When she stepped into the train station she began to get excited. Soon she would be home with her dad and Stormy. And she could stop lugging the saddle, which was so heavy her arms felt ready to drop off. To her dismay, the ticket office attendant told her the only train that could get her to Snake Hills that day had already left. The next one was at nine the following morning. She decided to buy her ticket now anyway, but the two-dollar fee to store her saddle was way over what she had left, a meagre eighty cents. She'd save that for a couple of bread rolls and lug her saddle. Oh well, there were plenty of drinking fountains around and water was all you needed to survive.

She thought of phoning her dad but realised he would probably be out mustering. At least by the time he got back she'd be there to surprise him. The prospect of spending a night under the stars appealed to her. She'd missed that at Thornton. What she had to do now was fill in her day.

᠌᠎ ᠎ ᠎

Leila abandoned ship, or the swimming pool at least, in the city. She stood among the speeding, noisy vehicles, the sound of rivet guns and sirens, and took a deep lungful of exhaust fumes. It wasn't L.A. but it was still dirty, noxious and wonderful.

Nobody even blinked an eyelid at her as she headed for the train station. Everybody had their eyes cast down at the footpath or stared ahead into nothingness. Finally one businessman did a double-take.

'Hey, that's a horse. Shouldn't we do something?'

The only people who paid him any attention were some kids on skateboards who explained to him it was obviously some hidden camera stunt for television and he'd just look like a doofus if he made a fuss. So the businessman shut up and Leila trotted on, unfettered.

Arriving at the train station, Leila headed for the ticket office but pulled up when she saw a cop there. She snuck behind a trailer load of luggage and listened as the ticket guy explained that a girl carrying a saddle had been through a couple of hours earlier and bought a ticket for Snake Hills. So the cops were looking for Charlotte. What if they found her? If they arrested her for stealing then she would never make the JOES and Leila would never be able to forgive herself. She had to find the kid before the cops and get her back to Thornton Downs to compete in the JOES trials. She thought hard. Imagine you're a country rube in the big city. You've got no money. Where are you going to head to fill in time before your train?

Charlotte lay on the grass in the sun, looking out at the yachts on the river. It was so pretty. She wished that her mum and dad could be here. All three of them again like those picnics they used to have. Of course, that could never happen now. She bit into the bread roll she'd bought and thought of Thornton Downs. Not a single person there would miss her. The only friend she thought she'd had, had turned out to be a lying sneak. For a little while there she had been happy, she'd almost imagined herself in the JOES. What a joke! She was disappointed she hadn't got to know Todd Greycroft better but it was too late to worry about that now.

Given time to kill, most kids Leila knew would go to some amusement parlour, but that didn't seem like Charlie's style. Maybe she'd go to a movie? Some sweet, sentimental thing that would make Leila puke.

Leila trotted down the street until she found a movie theatre. Before she had figured out how to ascertain whether Charlotte was there she noted that *Show Pony*, a film she'd completed last year, was playing, but only at the ten-thirty a.m. session.

What was this?

She couldn't wait to tell Mr Gold. How dare the exhibitors restrict her film to just one session. Just as Leila was contemplating what havoc to wreak on the cinema, a mother walked by with a kid, sucking on a milkshake.

'You want to see *Show Pony*, Chelsea?' asked the mother.

'*Show Pony* sucks. Everybody knows that.' The girl stated it with authority in between slurps.

Leila had a strong impulse to trample on the kid's fat foot. *Sucks?* What would this twerp know?

The mother was equally surprised.

'I thought you liked Sarah-Jane and Leila?'

'I hate that whiny Sarah-Jane. I'd like to smother her in honey and tie her over an ants' nest.'

Ah, the kid was discerning after all. Leila chuckled at the image she'd conjured many times herself.

'And what about Leila?' asked the mother.

Leila's ears pricked up, waiting for the inevitable compliment.

'Nah, Leila's a fake. She doesn't even do her own stunts.'

At that moment, her pride sinking through the floor, Leila felt the mother's eyes fall on her.

'My goodness! Isn't that Leila there?'

The kid shook her head.

'Nah, too skinny. These days Leila looks like a lifebuoy.'

Leila's legs wobbled. It was all she could do to stop collapsing. Was this what her public thought? Had Feathers been right all along? Oh, how she wished she had that bird brain there right now. Not only as a pal to support her emotionally in this dark hour but for practical reasons. He'd be able to do an aerial reconnaissance for Charlie.

But he wasn't there. Nor was her mother, or Tommy, or Charlotte. Leila felt suddenly more alone than she had in her whole life. Darn it, she missed the kid! Charlie had really cared about her. In Hollywood there were plenty of hangers-on who cared about you when you were hot but on the way down, oh, you'd be lucky to find a flea prepared to suck your blood. Leila had always known this, she'd just never considered the possibility that she might ever be on the way down herself.

One dumb no-neck bird, and one rube. Some fan club. And maybe by now Feathers had forgotten Leila anyway? She couldn't blame him. She'd taken him for granted, giving him constant lip. Despite that, he'd stayed with her. The fact he was stuck in a cage might have had something to do with that but Leila held a faint hope that maybe even if he hadn't been locked up he would have remained. By now, though, he'd probably found a new pal, one that was much nicer to him than she had been.

∽ ∽ ∽

On location in Hollywood, Bobby and Ralph were dismantling the special shower that Tommy Tempest had them set up for Leila. Ralph was really angry with Bobby. Firstly, his stupid idea of putting Leila in a paddock had cost him two million bucks. Now, because Leila had disappeared, the studio didn't even need to hire this shower from him. Ralph was broke and it was all Bobby's fault. He deliberately turned so the long steel pipe he was balancing on his shoulder swung around and clunked Bobby in the head.

'Ouch, watch it!'

'Sorry,' said Ralph, who wasn't sorry at all.

From his perch inside the trailer, Feathers saw the men dismantling the shower and couldn't believe his eyes. One of them was the nag-napper! And the other seedy guy was probably in on it too. But how could he prove it? He needed to get his wings on something incriminating, something he could get to Mr Gold.

That meant first he would have to get out of his cage.

# Chapter 12

It was a very sad Joel Gold who stared at the birdcage where Feathers lay flat on his back, legs in the air. Feathers had been the best employee he had ever had. Anything Mr Gold said, he said it right back, word for word – no rewrites, no smart ideas of his own. And now he was dead. Joel Gold opened the cage and gently brought Feathers out. He was still warm. He couldn't have been dead for very long.

'Guess I better find something to bury you in, old pal,' he said, placing Feathers on a table. He didn't notice Feathers' eyes flick open with concern at the word 'bury'! As soon as Mr Gold disappeared into another room, Feathers was up and out the window.

Mr Gold came back with an empty Moët champagne box. 'Here you go, Feathers, only the best –'

He stopped cold, flummoxed. Feathers was not there. He looked on the floor in case he had rolled off the table. Nope. It was the last straw. He was outraged. First they steal Leila, now Feathers. And Feathers was dead!!!

It was sick. Hollywood was turning into Hollywood.

ɔ ɔ ɔ ɔ

It had been many years since Feathers had been in the open air. Actually he preferred air-conditioned comfort to the smog, which could get so heavy it weighed your wings down. It was easy to get disoriented up there in the big blue of L.A. But all the same, it was nice to stretch the old wings.

It took him only a couple of minutes to locate the crims. They were loading pipes into the back of a truck. Feathers began circling, hoping to hear something incriminating, but they hardly spoke to one another. After about fifteen minutes his wings began to get very heavy. Just as he was thinking he would have to rest up in a tree somewhere, the suspects went to fetch more pipes.

Seizing the moment, Feathers flew into the back of the open truck. He had no idea what he was looking for. He just hoped there was something to link them to Leila; ideally, a photograph of them all together.

The back of the truck was filled with pipes and didn't seem to offer much hope, so he took a shot at the cabin, an absolute pigsty of fast-food wrappers, cookie boxes and empty soda cans. He tried the dashboard and the floor. Nothing.

He was about to check the glove compartment when he heard their voices getting closer. It was too late to escape so he flattened himself against the back of the seat. His plan was to take off when they went to the back of the truck but his plan hit the rocks when the fat one stayed by the cabin door while the other one shut the back. Now Feathers was terrified. They were getting ready to leave and he was trapped – red-winged, so to speak! Feathers had visions of them feeding him to some hungry Siamese. He couldn't help it, a little bird poo escaped. Why oh why did he have to be so stupid? What had Leila ever done for him anyway?

The one at the back was coming to the cabin. The driver's door handle started to turn. He was a goner! He held his breath. The handle turned . . .

. . . and stopped. Feathers continued to hold his breath. He could feel himself turning purple. He heard Ralph.

'You know, this is stupid. Instead of leaving now we should go back to the lunch cart and load up.'

Bobby pointed out they were no longer on the film payroll.

'The caterers don't know that.'

Bobby saw his point – free burgers and sodas, way to go. The two of them headed off. Inside the cabin, Feathers let out a loud sigh and gulped air. He had been lucky. Time to scram. He was about to do just that when he remembered he hadn't checked the glove compartment. He pressed in with his beak and it flipped open. A whole bunch of little papers flew out. Feathers flicked through quickly. Petrol receipts, betting tickets, but no photo.

Feathers was about to go but one of the receipts stuck to his wing. He tried to pull it off with his beak. Darn thing was all sticky. Candy and caramel. Finally he managed to yank it off. Then it stuck to his beak. He was trying to scrape it off his beak onto the wheel when some big grubby handwriting on the back of the docket caught his eye. He rolled his eyeballs around for a better look. It was kind of hard to read when it was right there on his beak, a little too close to focus.

And then he managed to read some of the poorly spelled words and his heart almost burst with happiness.

 っ っ っ っ

In the recliner in the trailer, Joel Gold was fast asleep, dreaming of awards he'd received with Leila and Sarah-Jane. The good old days. Then the dream vanished. Something was tickling his nose. Darn!

His eyes flicked awake and he gradually recalled that he had dropped off to sleep in the recliner. He pulled the irritant off his face. A piece of paper. Some inconsiderate flunky had left a memo on his moosh. Whoever it was, they'd be fired!

Gold studied the memo, looking for a clue as to the identity of the miscreant. He now saw it wasn't a memo but an invoice from RALPHS REMOOVALS AND PLUMMING. A blank invoice, not made out to anyone. Was this some sick joke? He started to screw it up.

Watching with horror from the cage, Feathers knew he had to act.

'Other side!' he whispered.

Joel Gold stopped. Had somebody spoken? He looked around him. No, the trailer was empty.

Just for the heck of it he turned over the invoice. He couldn't believe his eyes. Badly spelled in an ugly, dirty scrawl were the exact words the nag-nappers had spoken over the phone: 'Leev the monee in unmarked bills in the trash can by the Nantville exat Interstate 106.'

Was it a new message? No, this was what the nag-nappers had said. They must have read it off this piece of paper, which must have fortuitously blown in through the open window. The nag-napper could be this Ralph who couldn't spell removal or plumbing!

Joel Gold recalled the guy now. Yes, very shady, always hanging around the set with crocodile eyes. He jumped up, smiled at Feathers and ran towards the door waving the docket triumphantly.

'We got him, Feathers! We've got the nag-napper.'

He charged outside, closing the door. Feathers was elated. YES! His plan had worked. The door swung open again and there was a confused Joel Gold. 'Feathers? You're not dead?'

Feathers did his best to remain po-faced. Joel Gold slowly shook his head, muttered to himself and retreated again from the trailer.

# Chapter 13

Leila's hoofs hadn't been this sore since Hilary Duff's party when she and Paris had been literally dancing on the ceiling. In looking for Charlie, she'd decided to work out from the railway station a block at a time. She'd already covered about eight blocks on each side. This section of town was the pits. Greasy wrappers and crushed cans littered every inch of square space, provoking in Leila a strong recollection of being backstage at a heavy-metal gig.

By now afternoon was well and truly over. Street lights and neon signs were starting to poke out of the gloom. Why had she been so selfish? All night she'd been thinking of Charlie and the fun they'd had together and how Charlie had been a real friend to her. Like when Leila had messed up at the jump-off, Charlie's concern had been that Leila was sick. Leila wished she had come clean up front. Maybe Charlie had been the only chance at a true pal Leila would ever get?

Leila was peering down an alley when she heard something that scared her to the core – the sound of a twelve-year-old boy.

'Dad, look!'

The boy and his father were both staring at her. The father immediately began dialling his mobile phone.

'It's okay, Damian. I'll call the police.'

Leila had to act fast. She snapped at them.

'I'm not a horse, you idiot. We're actors dressed as a horse. Now get out of the way, you're wrecking the shot!'

Leila had noted many times that people had a much greater respect for movie-makers than police, and it was proved yet again. The father and son apologised and moved off rapidly. That was a close call. She trotted on. Charlotte had to be here somewhere.

ᴐ ᴐ ᴐ ᴐ

The sun had gone down and it was getting cool. Dark clouds loomed in the distance, pregnant with rain. Charlotte picked her way through the park looking for a place to sleep. The same park benches that had been filled with office workers and children earlier in the day were now taken over by people with missing teeth and wearing dirty woollen beanies. Some had covered themselves in old newspapers and hunched beside old boxes packed in shopping trolleys. Charlotte had assumed everybody in the city lived in a house but it seemed that these people were settling in for the night. Unfortunately, they didn't look very happy about it.

For the first time she doubted sleeping under the open skies in the city was going to be as much fun as it was in the warm, dry outback where there were only poisonous snakes to worry about. Charlotte decided to head for the rotunda in the centre of the park. At least there she would be covered if it rained. She was just starting to walk up the steps when a man's voice from somewhere in the dark called out.

'Where do you think you're going?'

She couldn't see anybody but she was ready to run just in case. The voice had sounded harsh and gravelly.

'Yes, you, girlie.'

Her eyes followed the sound. She caught her breath and almost choked. The man speaking to her was unshaven and dirty and lay on the rotunda roof.

'The rotunda is Mad Mike's spot, you'd best be getting home before he comes back.'

And now that Charlotte looked closely she could see that indeed there was a thin mattress and an assortment of garbage bags laid out in the shadows of the rotunda.

'Go on, girlie. Off you go.'

Charlotte didn't need any further encouragement. She ran as fast as she could while carrying the saddle over her shoulder. Whoever Mad Mike was she figured it was best to stay out of his way. She didn't slow down for at least ten minutes.

The new area she found herself in was deserted. It looked like some sort of construction site with big wire fences all around. Behind one of the fences was an area where old furniture and rubbish had been dumped. Charlotte could see an old sofa there. This time she looked very carefully for a sign of anybody. Nope, all clear. She heaved her saddle over the fence and climbed after it. Scattered around were some sheets of old tin that she could make into a shelter. The sofa had lots of stuffing missing but even so, it would be much more comfortable than a bench. Charlotte spent a few moments rigging the tin sheets into a lean-to and then climbed onto the sofa and lay her head on her saddle. She was so tired her eyes shut immediately.

She was drifting off to a deep sleep when the noise woke her. It was a low, building growl. Charlotte let one eye flick open. A huge dog stood a few metres away, pawing the earth, drooling. Charlotte liked dogs and most dogs liked her. Perhaps, despite his scary looks, he was just scared himself? Charlotte put on her best smile.

'Hello, fella. You're not worried about me, are you?'

The dog answered by baring its teeth. They resembled a set of knives stuck in the gums by the handle. This really wasn't going so well.

'Right, your spot. Okay, no worries, I'll leave it to you.'

Everything she knew about dogs told her it was getting ready to attack. Charlotte was trying ever so slowly to edge away. Just as she got to the end of the sofa, it charged.

She leapt for the fence. The dog shot up like a missile, missed her backside by a millimetre and snagged her plush toy horse in its vicious mouth. She and the dog fought a tug of war. When the dog let go for a split second to get a better grip, Charlotte took her chance, heaved the saddle over the fence and then scampered over herself. As soon as her feet hit dirt, she grabbed the saddle and ran, failing to realise that her special little horse had fallen off. All she could think about was putting as much space as possible between her and that vicious dog, which was still trapped behind the fence, barking loudly.

The saddle was heavy on her shoulder as she ran down a pitted bitumen road flanked by broken buildings. Judging from the faded sign writing on their brick walls, she guessed they must have been factories. Apart from the barking of the dog, thankfully growing more distant by the second, it was very quiet here. Not even the sound of traffic from the main road reached her. Then all of a sudden the sky lit up and there was an enormous clap of thunder. Big drops of rain began falling. She headed for the nearest building, an old brick warehouse. Its front door was padlocked. The rain was becoming heavier now. She looked up and saw a window on the first floor. If she could just make it up there . . .

She reached up and grabbed a drainpipe above her head. Would it hold her weight? There was no way to be sure but with the saddle still slung over her shoulder she grabbed the pipe with both hands and hauled up with all her strength, wrapping her knees around the pipe. Slowly she pulled herself higher. Eventually she could see the window above her.

Please, be open! She was nearly there when the pipe gave an ominous creak and began to pull away from the wall. It was a long way down to the ground below. Her hand shot out and reached the window sill. The window was closed. The pipe felt rickety, as if it could collapse any second. She got her fingers under the sill and pushed up. To her immense relief the window lifted. She heaved the saddle inside and rolled in after it.

The place smelled bad. It was pitch dark once you moved away from the window. Nervous, Charlotte swallowed hard. Could she spend the next eight hours here? Yes, she told herself, she could. Just then another huge clap of thunder sounded and she nearly jumped out of her skin. She quelled the urge to run. Where could she go anyway? She wished she had a light. She wished her father were there. But she didn't, and he wasn't, and she had learned a long time ago that it was no use trying to change what you couldn't. She'd just have to make do. Outside she heard a whoosh of rain. She was pleased she wasn't in the park.

Just as she was about to lie down she had the feeling someone was watching her from the dark interior of the bare room. Her skin crawled.

'Is anyone there?' she called out, trying to sound brave. Nobody answered. She strained to hear anything, remaining motionless for a long time. Not a sound came to her except for the rain and the rumble of thunder outside. Maybe she'd imagined it? Trying to relax, she stretched out on the floor. As she turned her head to the side she saw two little red dots in the dark close to the floor, drawing closer. She gasped and sat up. For a moment she was too scared to breathe. Then the red dots zoomed towards her, revealing a fat rat baring its sharp teeth. Charlotte relaxed and stifled a yawn.

'I've been dealing with poisonous snakes since I was five. You think I'm scared of a mouse? BOO!'

She moved her head suddenly at the rat, which turned tail and ran. Now maybe she could get some sleep! She lay on her back, closed her eyes and dozed.

Perhaps Charlotte would not have slept quite so well if she had been able to see the sign that had fallen off the building and landed in the dirt. It read, DANGER, DEMOLITION SITE. DO NOT ENTER.

Leila did not like rain. She couldn't think of the last time she'd got wet from anything other than a spa or shower . . . well, if you didn't count that pool party at Britney's. But what choice did she have? She needed to find Charlie. She'd lost track of how long she'd been walking but she knew it was hours since the sun had gone down. She was starting to wonder if this whole expedition was a ridiculous waste of time when she caught a break.

She was in a park with a lot of hobos scattered about. Most were snoring their heads off but there was one guy sitting up on top of a rotunda who seemed promising. Leila figured if the guy was sitting up on the roof of a rotunda in a storm, he wasn't going to be fazed by a talking horse.

'Say, Mac. You see a girl about thirteen come through here today carrying a saddle?'

The man nodded. 'Just before the storm. She went that-a-way.' He pointed.

'Thanks and God bless,' said Leila, excited by the information.

'Hey horse, can I ask you something?'

Leila stopped. One good turn deserved another.

'Are you really a talking horse or am I delirious?'

Leila lifted an eyebrow.

'If you were delirious, could you have imagined a horse this good-looking?'

The homeless man shook his head.

'There's your answer.'

At Thornton Downs Miss Strudworth spent another sleepless night. She was very distressed about the possibility of Charlotte Richards being alone at night in the city. Anything could happen to her. The police hadn't found her yet but they knew she hadn't boarded the train so she was there somewhere with the horse. The fact that she must have hidden in the bush near the stables and then come and taken the horse didn't endear Richards to Strudworth but even so, she could see the child must have been desperate. And now radio reports were coming in of a large electrical storm in the city. Miss Strudworth had tried to reach Charlotte's father but was told he was already on his way down for the trials. He was going to give Charlotte a surprise. He'd be the one on the receiving end of the surprise when Strudworth had to give him the horrible news that his only child was missing.

Miss Strudworth looked out of the window. Soon it would be light. They would be holding the dressage trials today. Normally she would be excited at this but not today. She just prayed Richards was safe for she couldn't help but feel that she had failed the child in some way. Life was harsh and Strudworth liked to prepare her charges for that reality rather than mollycoddle them and leave them vulnerable when they had to make their own way in life. But perhaps she could have and should have done more. After all, one was always learning. Strudworth prayed this lesson would not be too harsh a one for all concerned.

The truckload of men arrived at the demolition site as dawn was breaking. The foreman jumped out and told his men he expected them to be very careful, as they were dealing with dynamite.

'Lay the charges around the building and then take cover behind the truck,' he ordered.

The good part about the sun coming up was that it made it easier for Leila to try to spy Charlotte. Even so, thought Leila, it was like trying to find a needle in a haystack. Uggh, she shuddered at the thought. Chomping into a bale of hay and getting a needle in your mouth, what could be worse?

Ah choo! The sneeze came out of nowhere. It had stopped raining a while ago but . . . Ah choo! There was another one. Oh, and her nose was all sniffly. Just what she needed.

She had been trotting alongside a chain link fence, which isolated a block of bare ground inside it. Now she came to a point where a section of fence had been flattened. She stepped over it for a sticky-beak and saw what looked like a rubbish tip about a hundred metres in. Drawing closer, she saw somebody had made a shelter with tin sheets. She noticed something on the ground by the fence on the other side that gave her a jolt. It was the plush toy from Charlie's saddle. Leila's heart skipped a beat. She looked around. The kid must be here somewhere. 'Hey, Char-lie,' she yelled out. But her voice just echoed around the deserted buildings.

The foreman's name was Charlie too.

'You call me?' he asked his explosives man as he appeared at the truck rolling out a long explosives fuse that stretched all the way to a deserted factory.

'Nope,' said the explosives man.

'Okay then,' said the foreman. 'Let's start the countdown.'

Charlotte woke and stretched. Thanks to the sunlight streaming through the window she could now see her surroundings a lot better. It was simply a big bare room with a concrete floor and pockmarked brick walls. She checked her watch. Just after six a.m. Plenty of time to make the train. As she lay there hungry, she envisaged the other girls back at Thornton, full from a big breakfast, just leaving the stables now, getting ready for the dressage trials. She felt a pang of regret but put it out of her head. Sometimes it didn't matter how hard you tried, you didn't succeed. Look at her mum. She'd fought with every ounce of strength she'd had to beat the cancer that had put her in hospital but she didn't succeed.

She wished her mum were here. She wished she could hold her and feel her heart beating next to hers. Automatically her gaze travelled to her saddle, looking for the plush toy, but there was just a piece of ribbon dangling there now. She sank even lower, recalling the fight with the dog. It must have fallen off along the way. And then she started to cry. She had told herself she would never ever cry again. After her mum died she had cried for weeks. Sometimes it had seemed she would never be able to stop. But she had. Up until now. And here, out of nowhere, in the middle of nowhere, she was bawling her eyes out again.

Leila stood at the perimeter of the fence, scanning for any sign of life.

'Char-lie!' she called again. Nothing. She would have to find a way through the high fence on this side before she could investigate those buildings. As she was about to start off she heard a man's voice in the distance call out.

'Dynamite set.'

DYNAMITE! Leila looked over and saw the explosives crew donning earmuffs and taking shelter behind the truck. She noticed the foreman nod to another man who then lit a long fuse. The little sparking star began its snaking journey towards the derelict buildings.

♪ ♪ ♪ ♪

Charlotte forced herself to stop crying. It didn't help one bit. She was looking for something to dry her eyes with when she imagined she heard somebody calling her name. She shrugged it off. Then, there it was again. It sounded like . . .

No, it couldn't be! Leila?

Charlotte got to her feet and poked her head out of the window. In the distance was some sort of truck but there, just a few hundred metres away, Leila stood behind the wire fence. Charlotte blinked, suspecting she might be dreaming. But when she opened her eyes Leila was still there.

Charlotte felt warm inside. Low-down sneak or not, she'd missed her. She waved out the window and yelled.

ᴐ ᴐ ᴐ ᴐ

Leila followed the sound. Her eyes bulged from her head. There was Charlie! Waving from the building that was about to be blown up. A hollow fear gripped her. No point yelling at the crew, they were all wearing earmuffs. Leila's eyes travelled to the top of the high wire fence. It looked sharp. She would have to jump the fence but if she landed on it she'd be horse kebab.

Okay, it wasn't cardboard but nor was she some useless Hollywood bimbo. She was Leila, a star, descended from the greatest stunt horse and most athletic mare the world had ever seen, and she was the only chance Charlie had. Leila felt she had been born for this moment. She had to save Charlotte. If she could do that then maybe her selfish and shallow life wouldn't have been a complete waste.

She galloped fast at the fence, the fuse growing shorter by the millisecond, the fence looming massively ahead. Closing her eyes, she made herself think Tinkerbell, just like Charlotte had taught her. She pushed off with her back legs. Up, up, up she flew. The top of the fence passed under her, grazing her belly, but she cleared it and landed in full stride on the other side.

Her eyes flashed open. The moving spark was still running ahead of her. She reached it, trying to stamp it out, but with this darn cold her reactions were a fraction slow and she kept missing . . . and the fuse kept burning.

She yelled at the window for Charlie to jump but the kid had disappeared. The lit fuse was at her feet. The dynamite would blow any second. Leila tried the left hoof, missed, the right hoof, missed . . .

There was nothing for it. She sat her backside down on the fuse.

OUCH! That hurt.

She smelt burning flesh – hers! But finally the hissing stopped. She got up and confirmed the fuse had been extinguished. Phew.

Now Leila could see that the door was padlocked. Big deal. She turned and battered the door in with her sore rump. She found Charlotte waiting for her with a dopey expression on her face.

'Leila, what are you doing here?'

'Stopping you from making the biggest mistake of your – ah choo – life. Listen, I'm sorry about the pizza . . .'

Suddenly Leila was having trouble talking. In fact she was having trouble even breathing. She sounded like she'd swallowed a piano accordion.

Charlotte's face registered concern.

'That's a bad wheeze.'

Leila brushed it off. She couldn't afford to soak up the sympathy right now. 'Listen, we have to get back to Thornton. The trials will be starting in a few hours.'

'No. You're not well.'

'Hey, it's just a cold. It'll take more than that to kill me.'

From behind the truck the foreman and his explosives man scanned for a reason as to why the dynamite hadn't triggered. The dynamite man pointed.

'Fuse has gone out.'

The foreman was annoyed. He remarked that they would have to re-lay another fuse. But the dynamite guy smiled and held up a small gadget like a TV remote. 'No we don't. This is a radio remote. I can detonate by pressing this button.'

'Then do it,' said the foreman, taking his position behind the truck.

The explosives man pushed the button and dived for cover as a loud explosion ripped the building apart.

# Chapter 14

Ralph and Bobby were driven away, handcuffed, in a police car. Joel Gold looked after them sadly. So they'd got the bad guys. The trouble was, these klutzes didn't have any idea where Leila was. He'd been able to locate the property where Ralph and Bobby said they had left Leila but from there the trail went cold. The owners of the property shipped horses all over the world. That day alone there had been fifteen different shipments. Leila could be anywhere.

'She might even be dead, Feathers,' he said morbidly.

Feathers knew exactly how he felt. He felt the same way. All his good work had come to nothing.

ා ා ා ා

Inside the building where Leila and Charlotte had been standing was nothing but a sea of broken plaster and a cloud of dust. Of the girl and horse there was not a trace. Then a mound of plaster on the floor started to move and, like a crab emerging from the sand, Charlotte stood, caked in white plaster dust.

Her first thought was for Leila.

'Leila! Leila!'

She began clawing at the pile of debris.

A hoarse wheeze was followed by a spluttered reply. 'Over here.'

The voice came from behind her. She looked through the swirling mist to find Leila resembling a grey statue. Charlotte was so relieved. 'Oh, Leila.' She threw her arms around her.

Charlotte went to the ground floor window and looked out to find the cause of the explosion. There had been a building next door a moment ago and now there was just a pile of bricks.

'They've demolished the place next door,' she said.

She watched the workmen inspecting the hole in the ground. Looking satisfied, they climbed into their truck and drove off.

'We better split, and pronto,' Leila said.

'You're right. I've got a train to catch.'

Leila shook her head. 'No, no, no, no. The only place you're going is back to Thornton Downs.'

Charlotte folded her arms. 'I'm never going near that horrid place again.'

'Kill that attitude, sister. You belong in the JOES as much as any of those princesses. And if I'd been a better horse you'd be kicking their butt right now.'

'It doesn't matter what you say. It's too late.'

'It's never too late. We've got a few hours yet.'

But Charlotte was shaking her head. 'The police are looking for me. If they find me, they'll put me in jail.'

Leila shook her head. 'I'll confess.'

'Electrodes in the butt?' Charlotte reminded her.

Leila thought about that. 'I'll call Strudworth anonymously. Say The Evil Three made me do it.'

Charlotte shook her head firmly. 'No. The Evil Three might be spoilt conniving snakes but they're not thieves. Anyway, you've had a long trip. You need to rest.'

'Rest? I'm a Hollywood star. The only time I rest is on set. Let's go.'

'No way. I'm through with that place.'

Leila blew out through her nostrils. 'I can't believe you're scared.'

'I've killed snakes with my bare hands. I'm not scared.'

'You might be fine with snakes that slither along the ground but there are also snakes in designer frocks. You can't let a few spoilt brats take away what should be yours.'

Leila was annoying Charlotte. Possibly because deep down Charlotte knew there was some truth in what she said.

'You're the expert, are you?'

'I am ashamed to say I am. I've spent my life doing the same thing as them. When new actors turn up that might threaten me, I slip the hoof in. They're giving you a hard time because you're good. Maybe even better than them, and they want the JOES all to themselves. I believe in you, now you have to believe in you.'

Charlotte folded her arms. 'Nice speech. I guess you adapted it from one of your movies. Sorry, but I'm not going to be part of the JOES. It was a mistake. End of story.'

'Is that what you would tell your mom right now, if she were here with you in this room? That you couldn't stand the heat and wanted the easy way out?'

She sensed Charlotte's resolve wilting. Leila played her trump card. She dropped the plush toy down in front of Charlotte.

'Your mom led me to you because she knows you can't throw this chance away. Now shut up and climb on.'

In her heart, Charlotte knew that was what she wanted to do. She had just needed somebody else to push her. It was not just what her mum would have wanted, it was what *she* really wanted. She saddled up Leila and hauled herself up.

Leila cackled. 'Thornton Downs, here we come.'

From her vantage point by the judging post, Caroline Strudworth watched Lucinda complete a very strong dressage. A pity the girl's personality didn't match her riding. The crowd of parents and interested onlookers applauded from the temporary stands erected around the arena but it washed over Miss Strudworth, who was still worrying about Charlotte Richards. Mr Graham leaned over.

'Well, that's the last of them.'

Miss Strudworth took the microphone and began her well-rehearsed little speech. 'Ladies and gentlemen, thank you for your attendance. Tomorrow we will have the jumps . . .'

She faltered, barely able to believe her eyes. Cantering towards her across the arena was Charlotte Richards and Leila. A murmur went through the crowd at the late arrival. Miss

Strudworth waited, transfixed and deeply relieved.

Charlotte saw they had made the dressage in the nick of time. It had been several hours since they had set out from the city. First they had cut around its perimeter and then snuck aboard a freight train heading in the general direction of Thornton Downs. The train was slow but it afforded Charlotte the opportunity to change into her riding outfit and gave Leila the chance to rest. Her cough didn't sound good at all. The train got them within thirty kilometres of Thornton Downs. Leila had leapt from the train and galloped the rest of the way, without a word of complaint.

Looking across at the people in the stands, at Miss Strudworth, at the other girls lined up on their horses, Charlotte knew that Leila had been right. Charlotte had been running away. Not any more. If Leila could do this, so could she. Maybe she would fail but she was not going to quit, she would give it all she had. She owed that to her mum and dad, the people of Snake Hills, Leila, and most of all, herself.

She stopped before Miss Strudworth.

'We've been very concerned, Richards.'

'I understand and apologise, Miss, but I would like the opportunity to compete.'

Strudworth nodded.

'Very well. We'll discuss the other things later. What music do you choose?'

Charlotte handed over a second-hand CD, which at Leila's insistence she had purchased in the city with her last forty cents.

'Track four, please.'

Strudworth studied the CD, cocked an eyebrow and passed it across to the sound man. She picked up the microphone.

'Charlotte Richards will perform to *Vogue* by Madonna.'

Charlotte bowed to the judges and turned Leila around.

'Are you certain about this?' she asked Leila.

'I've danced to this in the Whisky, Studio 54 and the Viper Room. Just leave it to me.'

Charlotte looked at all the people looking at her and Leila and felt her stomach turn upside down.

'I'm so nervous,' she confessed.

'Nervous is waiting for the vet when you've got colic. Sit back, relax and let Leila do the walking. This is my turf.'

The music began and Leila started moving in a way Charlotte had never experienced. Leila seemed to float across the arena, stopping on beats, shimmying, twisting and flicking her legs at right angles. The gasps of the crowd were audible even from the middle of the arena.

Standing on the sidelines The Evil Three almost swallowed their tongues. They had never seen anything like it.

In sections where the music stopped and Madonna said 'Vogue', Leila literally stood statue-like in whatever pose she had just reached; leg up, leg down, neck twisted, even rearing on hind legs, perfectly rigid, for what seemed like an eternity. Each new stunt brought a more expressive sigh from the crowd. Eventually the music stopped, Leila did the splits and the crowd erupted rapturously. Charlotte couldn't believe it herself.

In all her years Miss Strudworth had never accorded top marks but she simply couldn't imagine a better dressage. The rest of the judges agreed. Mr Graham muttered it was a tragedy the girl would probably be expelled. Strudworth considered that.

'We'll see.'

Charlotte was dismounting, giving Leila a pat when she saw Strudworth looming.

'Marvellous effort, Richards. Truly the most

amazing dressage I have ever witnessed.'

'Thank you, Miss.'

Strudworth cleared her throat.

'I know it can be difficult coming from the outback to a place like this. If you apologise for taking the money . . .'

'I will not apologise. I didn't take the money and that's that,' snapped Charlotte.

Strudworth shook her head sadly.

'Very well. As you are aware the evidence against you is damning. You may continue to compete but I have to warn you, the JOES isn't just about horsemanship. It's as much about character and my decision will reflect that.'

Her excitement punctured, Charlotte watched Strudworth stride away.

Leila felt gutted. It was all her fault. No matter how well they did in the dressage or the point-to-point, Charlie was going to be blamed. She shuddered. She felt cold and weak all of a sudden.

'Are you okay?' whispered Charlotte, as if she could sense the problem.

'Nothing a choc-sundae wouldn't fix. Only joking,' Leila added.

Miss Strudworth was alone in the yard that evening, clearing up rubbish. She was distracted, wondering just how hard those girls had pushed Charlotte Richards. Perhaps the pizza business had been a cry for help?

'Charlotte Richards didn't take the pizza, I did.'

The voice, sounding like a young American woman, came out of the shadows. Strudworth couldn't think of any American girls in her squad. She peered in the direction of the voice and was startled when Charlotte's horse emerged.

ɔ ɔ ɔ ɔ

Dressed for bed in her pyjamas, Charlotte had been crossing towards the stables with a carrot for Leila when she'd heard Leila's voice. Leila? Talking? She changed direction and pulled up, horrified. Leila was in the yard *talking* to Strudworth. Oh, no! Charlotte ran.

ɔ ɔ ɔ ɔ

Miss Strudworth was so shocked to find herself being addressed by a horse, she found herself going along with it.

'You did?'

'Yeah, you see . . .'

Charlotte cut in, 'I can throw my voice.'

Strudworth's head whipped to Charlotte, who glowered at Leila, but Leila wasn't to be silenced.

'Charlie, stay out of this. I was to blame. I should take the rap.'

With a fixed smile on her face, Charlotte said firmly, 'Thank you, but I can handle this.' Before Leila could respond, Charlotte reached over and held Leila's mouth shut.

Miss Strudworth watched on, eyes bulging. Charlotte carried on.

'The thing is, Miss, I know stealing is wrong. But I never intended . . .'

Strudworth held up a hand.

'You don't need to explain. I understand a lot more now. Those girls you were rooming with were mean. I should have stood up to them on your behalf but I failed you. You were lonely, felt abandoned.'

Charlotte attempted to speak but once more Strudworth's hand shot up commanding silence. 'It's all right. I've been there. I've been the odd girl out all my life. You sought comfort food. It's understandable. The failing is mine, not yours. I'm sure from here on in you'll have no need for such behaviour.

Consequently, if you can qualify for the JOES, I will be delighted to endorse you.'

Later in the stable Charlotte admonished Leila for exposing herself like that. What if Charlotte hadn't shown up?

'They'd probably think Strudworth was a loony and you'd be home free. It was a can't-lose strategy any way you look at it,' Leila cackled, which set her off into a fit of dry coughing.

'I think I should get the vet for you.'

'All I need is a good night's sleep. You too.'

Charlotte kissed Leila goodnight and took herself off to bed. She was sure they had scored well on today's dressage – all they needed now was a solid round on the jumps and the point-to-point and she would be a JOE.

# Chapter 15

Charlotte was in the dining room, dressed for a day of jumping, about to scoff down a quick bowl of cereal, when Miss Strudworth burst through the door and came striding towards her. Charlotte's first thought was that Strudworth had changed her mind about the deal and she was back in trouble.

It was something far worse.

'I'm afraid it's Leila. She has a fever. The vet is with her.'

Charlotte didn't even feel the bowl slip from her hands. Before it hit the ground she was running.

Emma, who had been next in line, steadily poured herself a tomato juice and turned to Rebecca, who stood beside her, cramming a pastry into her mouth.

'Now, isn't that a shame.'

Charlotte swung into the stables, her heart bursting. She ran full pelt towards Leila's box, arriving just as the vet stood and closed his bag. He was talking to Bevans.

'I've done pretty much all I can. From here it's in the lap of the gods.'

'You mean Leila might die?'

The words ripped their way out of Charlotte's mouth. The vet turned and studied her. 'She's your mount?'

Charlotte looked down at Leila, who was curled in a heap on the ground. 'She's my friend.'

The vet gestured helplessly. 'I wish I could give you a better prognosis. She has a viral infection. It could disappear in forty-eight hours or it could kill her. I'm sorry.'

As he and Bevan moved off she heard him tell the foreman that she needed to be kept warm. Charlotte threw herself down and hugged Leila with all her strength.

'Come on, Leila. You'll be fine.'

But the horse's eyes were closed and from her body came a deep and steady wheeze. Charlotte felt big warm tears well up and fall. No, this couldn't happen. She had loved her mother and she had been taken from her. Not Leila too.

She felt a hand on her shoulder and looked up through teary eyes to find Strudworth looking down.

'I'm terribly sorry, Charlotte. I know what it's like.'

Charlotte recalled the stuffed horse in Strudworth's parlour. Was that the fate that would befall Leila?

Strudworth coughed deliberately and said gently, 'The jumps trials start in half an hour.'

Charlotte looked at her blankly. 'Obviously, I can't . . .'

'You are entitled to a replacement mount. Not the ideal situation, I grant you, but I'm prepared to let you ride my horse, Romeo.'

'But I couldn't . . .'

'It's quite within the rules. You have had no chance to organise a replacement. Romeo is very tractable.'

Charlotte continued to shake her head. 'I mean, I couldn't compete while Leila was sick in here.'

Strudworth sighed. 'Loyalty is a wonderful thing but I'm sure if Leila could talk, she would urge you to carry on and make the JOES.'

But the words were bouncing off Charlotte like hailstones on a tin roof. She shook her head furiously.

'No, I'm staying with Leila.'

'Charlotte, if you miss the hurdles you won't score any points. Your chances of making the JOES will be minuscule.'

'I don't care. I can't do it.'

Strudworth tried one last shot. 'Your father is coming down to see you ride. It was meant to be a surprise. He'll be here tomorrow for the point-to-point but if you're not jumping . . .'

'He'll understand.'

Mr Graham poked his head into the stables. 'Caroline, we need to go through these guidelines.'

'Yes, I'm coming.' Miss Strudworth looked sadly down at Charlotte. 'I have to go now but I urge you to reconsider. Don't throw away a career.'

Then she turned on her heel and Charlotte was left alone with Leila. She rubbed Leila's muzzle. She was burning up.

Charlotte stayed cuddled up to her for a long time. Exactly how long, she couldn't have said. She was solely focused on getting Leila well. It was probably about midday before she even thought about the trials again. The other girls had long since come and taken their mounts out. They would be competing right now. Charlotte had laid her jacket over Leila and now she placed a damp cloth on her brow.

Leila groaned.

'Water . . . I need water.'

Charlotte screwed up the wet cloth so some water dripped into Leila's mouth.

'Don't taste like Perrier. I gotta have Perrier, gotta have class . . .'

Charlotte lied. 'It's Perrier. The fever makes it taste different.'

Leila relaxed. 'Girl's gotta keep her standards up.' Then she let out a high, deranged giggle. 'Perrier, yeah. Perrier the derrière. My butt's too big . . . gotta watch that new Palomino filly, Chiquita . . . start out as your understudy, next thing they're the star and you're an extra . . . can't trust nobody . . . Hollywood . . . not real friends . . . No mom or dad. You gotta look out for number one. Nobody else will.'

Charlotte lay her head against Leila and pleaded with her mother, if she could hear her, to not let Leila die.

ↄ ↄ ↄ ↄ

Strudworth watched the last of the riders complete the jumps. Some of the girls had been of a particularly high standard but that hadn't cheered her one bit. All she could think of was what might happen to the Richards girl if Leila didn't pull through.

Her train of thought was broken by Mr Graham, approaching at a brisk walk. 'That's it, then?'

'Yes, that's the last of them.'

He could see she was worried. 'Still fretting about Charlotte Richards?'

'I can't help it.'

'Nonsense, Caroline. You did everything by the book.'

She felt like saying to Mr Graham that while that was true, sometimes it was wiser to not follow the book. But she did not say that. Instead she smiled bravely and said, 'I'll see you tomorrow for the dressage.'

⌣ ⌣ ⌣ ⌣

Leila had been rambling off and on in a delirium for a little while now. She started up again.

'I know I let you down, Mom. But see, I was frightened when you left. I was a frightened itty-bitty little foal. I played the brat for attention . . . and now, now I've been sent . . . I'm burning. Daddy . . . I wish you could help me, I wish I'd known you more but now here I am, roasting. Oh, it's soooo hot. Please, Daddy, save me . . . I'M SORRY.'

Charlotte leaned over and kissed her. Leila seemed to calm. Then her eyes found Charlotte and she smiled. Her breath stank badly but Charlotte said nothing about that.

'My angel. My guardian angel. Is that you?'

'It's me.'

'Thank God you're here,' she whimpered and drifted off to sleep.

Around sunset the other girls returned with their horses. Most of them poked their heads in and wished Charlotte good luck, but Emma, Lucinda and Rebecca kept their distance.

'It's her own fault,' whispered Emma in that superior tone of hers as they hung up their tack. 'The horses are there to serve us, not the other way around.'

Lucinda said she suspected it was all a con. 'Look at that pathetic effort against Milthorp. She's not very good at jumping so she piked out.'

Rebecca merely gazed at herself in the mirror hanging by the tack and wondered if her zit would go down in time for the dance with the Milthorp boys the next night.

Eventually they all shuffled off and Charlotte was back alone with Leila, just how she liked it. Around seven that night Miss Strudworth arrived with food for Charlotte. Charlotte told her she appreciated her going to the trouble but she wasn't hungry. Strudworth asked if she minded if she joined her.

'Of course not,' said Charlotte, but she was lying.

Miss Strudworth checked Leila's temperature and noted it was much the same.

'Can't we put her on a drip or something?' Charlotte wanted to know.

Strudworth explained the vet had said with this virus it was pointless. She began talking of her days as a young rider like Charlotte and how she had experienced a similar trauma with Zucchini. She had nursed him for three days after the vet had written him off. Eventually he came good. The story bucked Charlotte up.

'Unfortunately,' added Strudworth with gravity, 'we haven't got three days. Leila may recover but it will be too late for you.'

'Isn't it too late already?' asked Charlotte absently. She assumed she was already out of contention.

'If you win the point-to-point tomorrow, and only if you win, you would have enough points to qualify,' explained Strudworth. 'You owe it to your father, your town and yourself to have a go.'

'But suppose I did ride Romeo. Suppose I won the race . . .'

Strudworth, who saw this discourse as a positive step, was nodding along.

'And then I raced back here and something horrible had happened to Leila. How could I live with myself?'

It was then that Strudworth realised the futility of her mission. 'Very well, Charlotte. Have it your way. You may sleep the night here with Leila.'

Charlotte smiled a warm thank you.

The night passed slowly. Unwanted memories of a vigil by her sick mother's bed kept forcing their way into Charlotte's brain but she forced them right back out. She kept talking to Leila about all the fun they were going to have together. She reminded Leila she had promised to show her Hollywood and Charlotte told her one day she would show her Snake Hills. She tried to think of anything about Snake Hills she hadn't yet told Leila but in the end didn't worry if she was going over old ground. Leila couldn't really hear her anyway. Extremely self-conscious, Charlotte even hummed a few of Leila's favourite songs. Finally, in the darkest and stillest part of the night, exhausted, Charlotte's heavy eyelids dropped down and she fell asleep.

She awoke when a rooster crowed in the distance. She jumped up, remembering where she was, and thrust out her hand to feel Leila. Her heart stopped. Leila was cold. She had died in the night and

Charlotte had not even realised. Tears gushed. 'No, no, it's so unfair,' she wailed.

'What's unfair is a girl having to get her own drink. I'm parched.'

Charlotte turned but didn't dare believe. 'Leila?'

'No, Cher. Who do you think?'

Charlotte had never been so happy to hear one of Leila's smart-alec comments. She gave Leila water. Leila gulped it down and looked around.

'How long was I out?'

'A day.'

'A whole day?' Leila whistled. 'So, how did you go in the jumps?'

'I didn't.'

'You blew it?'

'No, I didn't jump. I wanted to be with you.'

Leila struggled to her feet. 'Tell me you're pulling my leg.'

But she knew from Charlotte's look this was no joke. She became agitated. 'What on earth were you thinking?'

'I guess that I wanted you to know that somebody was never going to desert you, no matter what.'

Leila felt herself choking up. 'Okay. Let's not try and shut the stable door after the horse has bolted. Can you still make the JOES?'

'Only if I win the point-to-point.'

'You're going to win the point-to-point.'

'Not possible. The rules state that if I had prior knowledge my mount was ill I have to give twenty-four hours notice. Yesterday I could take a replacement on the spot because I didn't know –'

Leila cut in. 'So you can't use another mount. You don't need another mount. You got me.'

'That's ridiculous. You're not strong enough.'

'I will be with you riding me. Now come on. I need to get some energy into me. Hit me with a Mars Bar.'

Charlotte smiled. 'You'll stop at nothing to get chocolate, won't you?'

# Chapter 16

Miss Strudworth had been forced many times to inform parents that their children, those little apples of their eyes, just weren't good enough to make the JOES. Somehow, no matter how difficult, she always found the strength. But here today, with Charlotte's father, a man who had driven more than a thousand kilometres in an old station wagon, she was finding it extraordinarily difficult to come to the point.

'Charlotte's been injured?' Tony Richards was trying to make sense of the woman's babbling.

'No, but her horse was sick. And that ruled her out of the jumps and, oh, this is all my . . .'

She noticed his attention leave her and a broad smile spread over his face. 'Charlie!' he called.

Strudworth turned around to see Charlotte trotting over on Leila.

'Hi, Dad.' She gave him a big hug.

'Miss me?'

'Of course. But Miss Strudworth has looked after me.'

Charlotte saw her father's look of disbelief. Strudworth's eyebrow shot up. Charlotte fired the quickest of winks to her. 'And this is Leila. She had a virus but she's all better.'

'Leila's a horse?' Her dad looked slightly baffled.

Leila felt Charlotte's dad's hand slide down her neck. Just like her dad would have been, strong and caring.

The other riders were moving past. 'Charlotte, you had better get to the start line,' urged Miss Strudworth. 'I'll look after your father.'

‿ ‿ ‿ ‿

A short time later the riders had lined up in a paddock, facing the bush. It wasn't dissimilar to the Golden Buckle race, thought Charlotte. The course took the riders from the paddock out into the bush through a cross-country course, before rejoining the paddock for the run home. The finish line was by the bleachers, where a sizeable crowd sat ready and waiting. Charlotte was too far away to pick out individuals but she knew her dad was there and she hoped, although she would never have said this out loud, that Todd might be too.

Further down the line, Emma sidled up to Lucinda and Rebecca.

'If Charlotte wins today, one of us could miss out on the JOES.' She wasn't telling them anything they hadn't figured out for themselves.

'We know.'

'Good,' said Emma. 'Then let's make sure she doesn't win.'

'Riders, ready!' commanded Strudworth.

'Sure you're up to this?' asked Charlotte of Leila.

Leila snorted. 'There's no limit to this little baby. You want soul, you get soul, you want action, you get . . .'

Before she could finish, the sound of Strudworth's whistle split the air and the horses sprang off. Charlotte spied an opening between Rebecca and Lucinda and sent Leila towards it, but Rebecca and Lucinda deliberately shifted in on their mounts and sandwiched her. Leila knuckled over, almost falling. It took Charlotte all her skill to keep her up.

In the stands the crowd let out a collective gasp. Watching through binoculars, an angry Todd shouted it was deliberate. The man behind him, Charlotte's dad, muttered, 'Too right it was.'

At ground level Miss Strudworth was thinking the same thing. And out on the course there would be many places where such tactics would go undetected.

She really hoped Richards and her mount could stand up to the treatment.

'Are you okay?' Charlotte called down to Leila as they entered the bush.

'I'm more than okay, I'm angry,' replied Leila.

They had lost substantial ground in the incident but Leila was already making it up on the tail-enders. She continued to make good progress, leaping logs and hedges, scooting fast down narrow dirt tracks. Pretty soon Charlotte and Leila had passed the stragglers at the rear and joined the middle group. Leila was feeling confident until she saw the tell-tale shimmer up ahead.

'Water! No way. I hate water, unless it's Perrier.'

'Just imagine it's perfume.'

Leila tried to pretend it was a big puddle of Tommy Girl. She jumped.

Splat! Into muddy water. That sure wasn't Tommy Girl.

Emma, Lucinda and Rebecca were right at the front of the pack. Emma looked back over her shoulder and yelled to the others that Leila and Charlotte were still there and making ground. Immediately The Evil Three slowed and spread themselves across the track.

Charlotte and Leila were at top pace as they rounded a bend where the track narrowed. Suddenly

Charlotte found three horses in front of her. There was no time to stop! Leila saw the danger too, and to avoid collision she scampered wide off the track, crashing through bush. Charlotte clung on for grim death. If Leila hit a rabbit hole here she would snap a leg. Leila was too angry to even think about that. She powered through the scrub and hooked back up onto the dirt track, further behind The Evil Three but intact. Once more she dug deep to pick up the gap.

Realising the threat, Lucinda dropped back. It looked like direct action would be needed. As Charlotte moved alongside her she raised her riding crop and brought it down over Leila's nose. Hard.

OWWW, that hurt. But Leila would not give up. Then she saw the crop raised again. Oh no! Wham!!! Down it came again, hard, right on her nose.

Leila's eyes were starting to water but she was determined. She saw the riding crop head towards her again – this time Leila was ready. She grabbed it in her teeth and yanked hard. Lucinda had no chance. The power of the horse pulled her right out of the saddle. She sailed through the air towards a stinging nettle bush . . .

つ つ つ つ

Charlotte concentrated on the drumming of Leila's hooves. She was focused on the remaining two horses up ahead. Any moment the bush would give way to paddock for the run home.

Leila could almost taste victory. The rumps of the other two horses were not far away now and she was closing. But as they breached the bush and landed on grass, she felt Charlotte ease off.

'What are you doing? I'm not tired, we can catch them,' she yelled.

'Not yet,' replied Charlotte. 'This straight is longer than you think.'

In the stands Mr Graham saw Leila losing ground and commented to Miss Strudworth that it looked like a race in two now.

Miss Strudworth reluctantly agreed. It appeared Richards' horse had run out of puff. Not surprising considering how sick it had been. Looking over their shoulders at the receding Charlotte, Rebecca and Emma believed it too.

'She's finished,' said Emma, matter-of-factly. 'Just you and me.' And with that she drove her horse forward. Rebecca went with her.

Behind them Leila watched the others pull away. 'We gotta go!'

'Not yet,' said Charlotte, with icy calm.

'We'll be too late.'

Charlotte reiterated more firmly. 'Not yet.' She knew that Leila would have to be nursed for one final effort.

For you, Mum, she thought, as she reached down and rubbed the toy horse on her saddle.

In the stands people were on their feet as Emma and Rebecca charged towards the finish line at least six lengths clear of Charlotte. Tony Richards understood Charlotte's tactics – after all, he'd taught them to her – but now even he was worried she had left it too late.

Charlotte calculated the distance to the line. She knew the breeze would be starting to work against the girls in front. 'Now,' she commanded Leila, pushing her with her hands and heels. Leila needed no further invitation. She switched on the turbo.

His heart sinking, Todd watched Emma and Rebecca charging at the line, hardly a breath separating them. And then his eye caught Leila powering out of nowhere like a jaguar, picking them up with every stride.

Rebecca and Emma literally heard the ground shake. They looked across and saw the looming shadow.

'Come on, you lazy nag!' yelled Emma, thrashing her grey horse with her crop. But her horse was tired and not inclined to help her. Rebecca's was even more tired. Charlotte gathered them in a stride. Leila put her nose in front and won!

In the stand the crowd was cheering. Loudest of all were Todd and Mr Richards as they both punched the air in triumph. Neither could have been more excited if he'd won himself. Even Miss Strudworth was jumping up and down and squealing like a schoolgirl.

As Leila and Charlotte slowed down past the finish line Leila said, 'Don't you dare tell people we won by my nose.'

Charlotte laughed and wheeled Leila around where they could bathe in the applause of the crowd. She patted Leila on the withers.

'Hey, we did it.'

Leila suddenly felt very, very, very tired.

'I need a drink,' she mumbled, before flaking flat on her tummy.

# Chapter 17

When the head honcho of the JOES announced 'Charlotte Richards' as one of those who had made it into the elite development squad, Leila's heart burst with pride. The rube had made it, no small thanks to Leila herself, of course. As she watched Charlotte's dad in the stands clapping his hands raw, she felt a pang of regret that her own mom wasn't there to see how well she'd done.

Some of the girls who'd missed out on the JOES were in tears. Looked like acting wasn't the only rough game in town. A pity The Evil Three had all made it through as well. Charlotte might have their measure in the arena but there was a dance on tonight and that was a different ball game entirely. The kid was going to need all the help she could get.

ↄ ↄ ↄ

It was a marvellous, still night. Insects swarmed around the Tahitian torches that lined the driveway, leading up to a dance floor where Thornton girls in expensive evening wear shimmied with the boys of Milthorp, dressed in their finest formal wear. A tuxedoed band played on a large platform out the front of the main building. Miss Strudworth and Mr Graham circulated among their charges to make sure everyone behaved themselves.

Spying Todd at the punch bowl, Rebecca flounced over in her designer frock and addressed him like an old friend.

'Todd! Great to see you here.' His curious expression forced her to add, 'Rebecca. We met at Ashleigh Rablestone's christening.'

Todd wondered what on earth she was on about. He said he only remembered being at Ashleigh's place for a pool party.

'That's right. The christening was when Ashleigh drove her new four wheel drive into her swimming pool and we all took turns sunbathing on the roof.'

Todd couldn't think of anything more moronic. He explained he'd already left before all that stupid stuff. Rebecca nodded like a bobbing dog on a car dashboard.

'It was stupid, wasn't it? She should have sunk it in

the deep end. Then her parents would have thought she'd just misplaced it.' She tutted and shook her head.

By now Todd was wondering if Rebecca had recently been released from some mental institution. He smiled wanly and tried to escape her by circling around the other side of the punch but she clung on, asking him whether he thought fake tan was preferable to a solarium-acquired tan. Todd ignored her question and asked one of his own.

'Is Charlotte Richards about?'

Rebecca sighed, and shook her head.

'Charlie? She's like, such a waste of space.' At which point her phone beeped. She checked its screen. *TIMEZUP BUTT OUT* appeared. She looked over to see Lucinda and Emma about twenty metres away, glaring at her. She turned back to Todd, fanning herself.

'It's so-oo hot. I'm going to cool off down at the creek. Feel free to join me.' She laughed before slinking off.

Todd felt a great wave of relief. Finally free of that . . . *thing*! But when he looked up, another Thornton girl with perfect hair and wearing an expensive dress was heading his way. Except for Charlotte, these girls all looked like they'd been poured from the same mould. They talked the same, too. He sighed. Why wasn't she here?

ɔ ɔ ɔ

In the stables, Leila studied Charlotte with a thoughtful expression on her long face.

'It's not that bad.'

Charlotte flapped her arms in her hideous dress. With no make-up and her hair tangled and lifeless on her shoulders, she felt like an old bride dolly that had lain for years in a shed under a pile of dusty magazines.

'I look ridiculous.'

'Noooo,' neighed Leila, unconvincingly.

Charlotte reminded Leila she had promised she wouldn't lie any more.

'Okay, you look like a generic cereal box when the printer ink ran out,' confessed Leila.

'Thank you.'

'But this is where a girlfriend can help. Especially one who's spent half her life in the make-up trailer.'

Charlotte was sceptical but Leila promised she could deliver.

'A little foundation to start.' She put her snout into her feedbag and emerged with a tube in her teeth.

'I took a stroll through the Ladies Restrooms during the presentation speeches.' She passed it to Charlotte, together with a small hand mirror. 'Now, a little on the back of your hand, then blend.'

Charlotte did as she was told. Next Leila dipped her tail into a small tub of blusher.

'Just a hint,' she explained, before slapping her tail lightly across Charlotte's cheeks. She reached back into the feedbag again and dropped a small tube of lip-gloss into Charlotte's hand. Charlotte applied the pale pink gloss. Leila checked her out like a doctor looking for skin cancer.

'Perfect.' But her lip curled as she studied Charlotte's hair. 'Now, that birds' nest. There's a big tube on the bench. Put a dollop on your hands, turn your head upside down and rub it through your hair.'

Charlotte did as she was told and was surprised to find her hair was now much thicker and even curly! She was thrilled.

'Is this what they call gel?'

'I guess. It's what the vet uses for internal examinations.'

Charlotte managed to avoid throwing up. But only just.

Unfortunately, there was still the sack she was wearing. Before she could utter a word, however, Leila had seized it in her mouth and began ripping. It scared the daylights out of Charlotte.

'What do you think you're doing?!'

Leila spat out material. 'Keep still.' She ripped again and again.

Charlotte couldn't see what was happening and was frightened to look.

'Do you know what you're doing?'

'Does Stella McCartney?'

Charlotte had no idea who she might be. Leila was talking at her again.

'Now listen up. It's a jungle out there. Those girls will try and tear you to shreds.'

Another rip, another spit. 'You have to use wit, not muscle. Got it?'

Charlotte shrugged. Leila finished and appraised her work.

'How do I look?' asked Charlotte anxiously.

'Good as possible with two legs missing,' replied Leila, using her tail to dust off a mirror hanging on the wall.

Charlotte gasped at her reflection. Was it really her? She couldn't believe she could look so hot.

'Told you,' said Leila smugly. 'Now go get 'em.'

Emma was having no more success with Todd than Rebecca had. Assessing early on in their conversation that Todd was the serious type, she was now trying to impress him with her political nous, explaining how she believed world peace could be achieved if only everybody could be made to watch *Charmed* three times a day. She noticed his mouth drop open.

'Wow,' he gasped.

Good, she'd finally got through. Emma was so rapt in herself she hadn't realised that Todd's eye line was straying over her shoulder to where Charlotte stood at the stable entrance.

'Exactly. It's amazing. I'm amazing,' announced Emma. And then she realised Todd was no longer standing in front of her.

 COCO

Charlotte could barely breathe. Her feet seemed planted in concrete. Todd Greycroft was advancing towards her. I'm not ready for this, she was thinking. But the next thing she was lunging to meet him. Leila had nudged her into the yard proper. Todd broke into a handsome smile.

'Hi.'

Todd was suddenly yanked back by a determined Emma.

'So world peace would be easy if people just weren't so *selfish*.' She glared at Charlotte. Emma herself was then suddenly pulled away and Lucinda stood in her place preening.

'I couldn't agree more. Hi, Todd. I'm Lucinda.'

'Nice to meet you.'

Todd shook her hand and turned right back to Charlotte, leaving Lucinda stunned. He started over again.

'That was a great ride today.'

'You were there?' Charlotte hadn't seen him, though she had looked hard.

'I had to go back to Milthorp to get ready. I tell you, it was almost like you were talking to your horse.'

Charlotte was surprised to find herself at ease talking with him.

'More like she was talking to me.'

Behind them Emma and Lucinda were equally outraged.

'That little nobody!' seethed Emma.

'Who does she think she is! Boy, is she going to get her just desserts,' hissed Lucinda, heaping ice-cream and custard into a bowl.

'How's the ankle?' Charlotte asked.

Todd grinned. 'Good for dancing.'

Carrying the bowl heaped with custard, jelly and ice-cream like it was a bomb, Lucinda zeroed in fast on Charlotte. She pretended to trip, tossing the dessert all over Charlotte.

'Oh, Charlotte! I'm so sorry,' she gushed, with not an ounce of sincerity. 'I slipped.'

Charlotte balled her fists, ready to pound Lucinda. But then she remembered Leila's advice about beating them at their own game. She forced a smile.

'Don't worry about it, Lucinda. But I'd go easy on those zit creams you use. They say the shakes are a common side effect.'

She saw she'd scored. Lucinda's face contorted into an ugly mask. She turned on her heel without a word and left the scene. Meanwhile, Todd had whipped out his handkerchief and started wiping the dessert off Charlotte.

'I thought you were sweet enough already,' he cracked.

Charlotte joined in the joke. 'Looks like dessert is on me.'

Charlotte dipped her finger in the remnants of custard and ate a little, making Todd laugh more. Charlotte liked Todd. He was fun to be around.

The retreating Lucinda found Emma waiting, laughing at her.

'That zit-cream gag was pretty funny.'

'So's this.' Lucinda picked up a custard tart and whacked Emma in the face with it. Emma grabbed a handful of jelly and rubbed it in Lucinda's hair.

'You *skank*!' shouted Lucinda.

They grabbed each other and fell to the ground, fighting.

'You take that back,' snarled Emma.

'Or what, Emma? You're going to throw my boots up the tree like you did Charlie's?'

Emma bent Lucinda's hand back.

'Take it back or get used to drawing your cartoons with your mouth.'

Two sensible brown shoes came into focus beside them. The girls stopped wrestling and looked up to see Strudworth peering down.

'I might have known,' she said, with thinly veiled disgust.

Meanwhile out on the creek-bank, Rebecca shivered in her bikini, fanning herself as if she was on the beach, saying loudly in the hope Todd might be nearby, 'It's so-oo hot here.'

Todd, however, was not nearby. He was having a great time dancing with Charlotte. When the band leader announced it was the last song, both he and Charlotte were equally disappointed.

'I had a great time, Charlotte,' Todd said as he waited to board the bus, which was taking all the boys back to Milthorp.

'Me too.'

He was the last on the bus, still waving to her as the door closed. Charlotte waved back. She felt a little giddy but in a good way. As the bus pulled away down the drive Charlotte thought of the fun they would have riding together in the JOES. She'd have a real friend here. Unfortunately, not her *best* friend. All of a sudden she was very, very sad

ᗡ ᗡ ᗡ ᗡ

It filled Leila with satisfaction as she watched the Milthorp bus pull away. Mission accomplished. She'd been so happy that Todd had taken an interest in Charlotte and Charlotte had done herself proud, matching every move those three little witches had made.

'Leila!'

The excited man's voice sounded familiar. Leila shot a look over her stall door. No! It couldn't be! But it was. Tommy Tempest and Joel Gold, big smiles on their dials, laden with pizza, were moving towards her.

Leila realised she had been so carried away with the actual event today she had forgotten all about Hollywood and mugging to the camera. How had they found her so quickly? But even as she asked herself the question she knew there was only one answer. Charlotte!

She reflexively swung to look back out her window. Charlotte was standing there beneath the moonlight staring back. Then she turned on her heel and moved off.

Leila sniffed the heavenly odour of pizza as Tommy shoved boxes under her nose.

'Here you go Leila. Hawaiian, Three Cheeses, Mexicana.'

Joel Gold unfurled a movie poster.

'And check this out! The poster for your next movie: *Stirrup and Pancake*.' Leila noted right away her name was double the size of Sarah-Jane's.

Gold was like an excited kid. 'Sarah-Jane kicked up a fuss but I said, GET OVER IT. Leila's the star!'

Tommy was telling her she was gonna love *Stirrup and Pancake*, a film about a young rider who becomes a Broadway star. Leila was overwhelmed. It was like all her dreams had come true.

In her room Charlotte lay on her bed telling herself she had no right to get upset. After all, she had come to Thornton Downs to make the JOES and she had succeeded. She had called the Hollywood people after the dressage. That had been the deal. Leila had kept her part of the bargain and it had been up to Charlotte to keep hers.

She wished her father were there to console her but he was staying in town. Anyway, she had to get used to dealing with this stuff by herself. Her dad wouldn't be around next term. Neither would Leila. In Todd, she would have a friend in the squad, that was something. She sighed. Todd was nice but he wasn't Leila. If only . . .

She stopped herself. She couldn't wish that Leila didn't go back. That was Leila's life and in life you had to do what you were born to do. She would just try and be happy for her.

The next morning in the stables, Charlotte brushed Leila for what each knew would be the last time. Leila had told Charlotte all about the new film and Charlotte had made all the right noises, doing her best to appear brave.

'We had some fun, didn't we?'

'Yes, we sure did, kid.'

Charlotte felt there was something she had to say before they parted company. 'I'm sure your mum would like to hear from you.'

'Nah. She doesn't care.'

'Of course she does. You know when you had that fever, you rambled on about how you wanted her to forgive you.'

'Yeah, well, I was delirious,' said Leila defensively.

'Just because she got it wrong sometimes, doesn't mean she doesn't love you. Look at my dad. The dress he had made for me was so gross I could've worn it to the Oscars.'

Leila couldn't help herself, she laughed a kind of wheezy cackle. 'Hey, not bad. I tell you, Charlie, you surprise me, you've got a sense of humour after all.'

Charlotte knew if she stayed any longer she would burst into tears. 'Well, I had better go and pack.'

Leila nodded. 'If you're ever in Hollywood . . .'

'If you're ever in Snake Hills . . .'

They stood in awkward silence, then Charlotte hung the brush up, kissed Leila on her nose for the last time and walked away.

She didn't see the big tear spill from Leila's eye onto the hay.

'There must be onions somewhere,' muttered Leila to the grey mare, who gazed across from her stall.

Strudworth watched the ritual of parents picking up their children, a number of whom would soon be back as JOES elite-squad members. Others would sell their ponies and move onto some other dream.

She was looking forward to young Charlotte reaching her potential. That girl could go to the very highest level. Her eyes flicked to where that nice producer, Mr Joel Gold, was loading Leila into a horse trailer. Pity in a way that Richards couldn't keep that horse. Strudworth had expected to see Charlotte there to farewell Leila but she was nowhere to be seen. Possibly too upset. Strudworth recalled how she had felt when she'd lost Zucchini.

Mr Gold waved, told Miss Strudworrth she was welcome any time at his villa in Malibu, climbed into his car and away they went. Miss Strudworth turned back to the large manor house. It would be much quieter with the girls gone. And much lonelier. Still, there was always a pack of cards waiting to play Patience with her and a good book to be read.

From the deserted bleachers, a red-eyed Charlotte watched Joel Gold's car and horse float travel down the drive and turn out onto the open road. 'Goodbye Leila,' she whispered.

Charlotte's legs felt rubbery as she traced the course where they had so often worked together, between flags, around rubber tyres, over hurdles. She had one hour before her father would pick her up to drive back to Snake Hills and, as she was already packed, she decided to go for one last walk through the bush where she and Leila had spent so many fun hours.

She walked up towards the top of the ridge, picking her way through wildflowers that today had no scent. Branches scratched at her but she didn't notice. All she could think of was Leila. She kept telling herself that Leila would be having fun soon in Hollywood and that was a good thing, but in her stomach she didn't feel good, just sick. About halfway up the ridge she stopped cold.

Right on top of the ridge, backlit by the sun, she could see a riderless horse. For an instant she thought it was Todd's horse, Warrior. The horse began to move towards her and when it dropped beneath the glare of the sun she was able to discern it wasn't Warrior, but a gorgeous bay mare. It tossed its mane. That mane! There was only one like it.

'Leila!' she shouted, and began running as fast as she could.

Just as excited, Leila galloped down the hill towards Charlotte. They met halfway and Charlotte threw her arms around Leila's neck and hugged her tight.

'What are you doing here?'

'The contract wasn't right. They were giving Sarah-Jane top-billing.' She hoped the kid couldn't tell it was a lie.

Charlotte said she was surprised Mr Gold would leave Leila after coming all that way to find her.

'Sometimes you have to bite the hands that feed you,' said Leila modestly.

In fact that had been exactly what she had done. Bitten both Tommy and Mr Gold at the first stop for gas. She'd also chewed on some soap to make it look like she was mad and frothing at the mouth. After that they decided they would use computer animation to recreate her for her next film and drove her back to Thornton Downs. She hoped she hadn't hurt them too badly. She liked them both but for now, she wanted to be here with Charlotte. Hollywood would still be there in a year or two.

# Chapter 18

A week later, Charlotte and Leila were riding on the thick red earth high above Snake Hills. During her first few days there, Leila had whinged constantly about having to rough it, but Charlotte had indulged her with ice-cream and that seemed to settle her down.

When Leila had asked Charlotte to call Mr Gold's number in Hollywood, Charlotte had thought Leila was going to ask to come back. But when the answer machine clicked on, Leila shouted for Feathers to pick up if he was there. After a moment of clattering and squawking, a rough voice came on the line.

'Leila, is that you?'

'Who else would it be, you lump of feathers? How's it going?'

Feathers explained that things were back to normal. 'Sarah-Jane is doing a new movie.'

'Did Chiquita get my role?'

'No. No horse this time. Joel and Tommy said horses are too difficult.'

Leila had muttered at that. Feathers continued, 'It's a pirate movie and guess who's playing the parrot?'

'You?'

'Yeah, I've got your old trailer. Hey, your mom has been asking about you, she's worried sick. I gotta go, somebody's coming. When are you coming back?'

'I don't know. When I'm ready.'

The two old friends said goodbye with promises to keep in touch and Leila seemed chirpier afterwards.

'I need you to do me a favour,' Leila asked Charlotte.

'No ice-cream before midday, you know the rules.'

'Na, something else. I jotted a postcard. To Mom. I tried to put the stamp on but it keeps sticking to my tongue. Hooves ain't the most useful things, some-times.'

Charlotte was thrilled. 'I'll put the stamp on and post it for you.'

Before she could tell Leila how proud of her she was, the air was filled with a massive roar. Looking up, they were shocked to see a low-flying cargo plane heading straight for them. For an instant Charlotte had thought it was going to crash on top of them but its silver skin passed over their heads and it touched down on the long, flat cattle track about a kilometre north, where it skidded to a halt, throwing up huge plumes of red earth.

Charlotte and Leila galloped over, assuming there must be some problem. Although prize bulls were often flown in by cargo plane, the planes always used the airstrip on the western edge of town. As Charlotte and Leila reached the plane the cargo hold slid open and a gangway rolled down from its belly. What happened next very nearly had Charlotte falling off.

Who should appear but Todd Greycroft, riding Warrior.

'What are you doing here?' Charlotte realised that was a pretty rude greeting but she was so shocked it was what came out.

'My dad owns lots of planes and I seemed to remember we had a challenge about a race.'

Charlotte laughed. 'So we did.'

Todd patted a picnic basket that balanced on his lap. 'I've a few hours before I have to head back. Thought you might fancy some lunch.'

While Todd and Charlotte caught up over lunch, Leila and Warrior warily circled one another. He whinnied in horse that just because Leila had fooled Todd didn't mean she'd fooled him.

'You might have cute fetlocks but you ain't no real horse,' he snarled, haughtily.

Leila shot back in human tongue.

'I'm too much horse for you, fella.'

The stallion replied in horse. 'That so? Let's see what you got.'

She would show him all right. She cleared her throat and tried to whinny. Nothing came out. The stallion turned away in disgust. Leila snapped.

'Wait up. I was just warming up.'

He rolled bored eyes at her. Right, that did it!

From somewhere deep inside came an instinct she didn't even know she had. She reared on her hind legs, pumping her forelegs and whinnying loud and clear. Warrior was amazed. He'd never seen a mare do that before.

Todd and Charlotte sat on the bonnet of the old car wreck, looking over at the horses.

'Looks like Warrior and Leila are getting on,' offered Todd.

'She can be charming,' replied Charlotte with a knowing smile.

Todd was smitten. That smile of Charlie's was a killer. He leaned towards her. 'You know, Charlie, you have the most beautiful . . .'

But before he get out the word, Charlotte shouted, 'No, Todd!' and shoved him hard. He fell off the car backwards and landed in the dirt. He was beginning to think Charlotte hated him when he saw her bend down to where he'd been sitting and yank a wriggling snake from the car body. With a quick flip of the wrist she dashed it against the car with a crack. She tossed away the lifeless reptile, smiling apologetically.

'Deadly brown.'

Todd nodded, slowly. Wow, what a girl!

Leila turned to the stallion. 'And I taught her everything she knows, so you treat me with respect, buster!'

The sun was about level with the ground when Charlotte mounted Leila. Todd was already on Warrior.

Charlotte turned to him.

'You ready?'

This was a girl who spoke his language! For an answer he yelled and set Warrior off down the hill. Charlotte and Leila responded immediately.

The competition had just begun!

## Acknowledgements

The late and very great Johnny Leopard, a wonderful comic who inspired me to go the extra furlong with Leila, who he helped create; the Random House gang of Zoe Walton, Chris Kunz and Ashleigh King for plaiting the tale; Rachel and Rick at Rick Raftos Management for all their help along the way; Sue Murray and June Jones for valuable feedback; and Mr Ed for setting the pace.

## About the Author

Dave Warner is the author of six novels and five non-fiction books for adults. He originally gained national recognition as a musician and songwriter, with eight albums to his name, but more recently music has been secondary to Dave's career as a writer for television and feature films. He lives in Sydney with his wife, two daughters and a son.

www.davewarner.com.au
www.charlotteandthestarlet.com

---

### Charlotte and the Starlet 2: A Friend in Need
Available now at all good retailers.

---